# HORROR
## ON THE HIGHWAY

Traveler stopped the van and stared at the road.
It was buckling, falling like stretched dough as
someone beneath removed support beams.

They leaped up now, and he had a blurry impression of them coming at him. He almost
gagged. They were mutants—what roadrats
called Bloats. Swollen, misshapen, squat like
dwarfs, but most of them were seven feet tall.
It was the extra holes in their heads that made
them hard to look at—inch-wide holes like pointless nostrils scattered about the skull . . . bubbling with pus and froth, or flickering with tiny
pink tongues.

Their eyes drooped unevenly, yellow-filmed and
owl-round. Their hands were big as shovels and
wickedly taloned. They were cunning, and industrious when they wanted to be. And they were
always hungry—for human flesh.

## TRAVELER #3

# THE STALKERS

## D. B. Drumm

A DELL BOOK

Published by
Dell Publishing Co., Inc.
1 Dag Hammarskjold Plaza
New York, New York 10017

Dell ® TM 681510, Dell Publishing Co., Inc.

ISBN: 0-440-18107-0

Printed in the United States of America

First printing—September 1984

DD

# 1

## The Bloats

He moved across the land like a ricocheting bullet.

Traveler drove the Meat Wagon, the sleek black armored van, at top speed, across the post-holocaust wastelands of the Southwestern United States, almost always in a straight line—till he came to an obstacle. And then he crashed through it or rebounded from it. Like a ricocheting bullet leaving something smashed where he'd struck . . . and speeding onward.

And he knew that sooner or later a ricocheting bullet runs out of momentum. Ends up buried in the earth, flattened.

But there was no use thinking about that. When your number's up, it's up.

It was a hot June day in what had once been central Nevada. There was no Nevada anymore, because there was no state government. They were all dead.

Most of the nation had died, fifteen years before, in the Nuclear Holocaust that had pretty much put an end to civilized life in the Northern Hemisphere.

The roads were still there—some of them. Cracked, fissured, interrupted, but still pulsing with traffic. The pulses, to be sure, came like the pulse of a dying man. In fits, trailing out. But now and then there was life, of a sort. A scrofulous, hungry, crazed sort, most of it, like the roadrats, the madmen who lived nomadically along the roads, resembling Indians gone punk, heavy-metal savages; preying on those who tried to survive in the few tiny clots of semicivilized order remaining. Torturing, brutalizing, trying to project the horror that had eaten up their own sanity onto the world around them. And there were other things, worse things, stalking the road. . . .

As Traveler was about to find out.

Traveler stopped the van in the middle of the road. The long cape of yellow dust behind the Meat Wagon overtook it and billowed like a djinn overhead as he climbed out of the cab, a 12-gauge pump in the crook of his arm.

He wasn't a tall man. Five nine, five ten, thereabouts. He was lean and cat-limber and strong with the strength of long endurance cut with burning inner intensity. His depth-less blue eyes and rugged, weatherbeaten, strong-jawed face told you nothing about what was going on in his head. Unless he wanted you to know something. And even then you might see only a flicker. But he had human feelings all right—locked up in him, in a steel safe that was his soul—in a safe to which he had long ago forgotten the combination.

Today he wore a flak jacket—like the one he'd worn on Long Range Recon Patrol sorties, fighting in Central America, two decades before—along with combat pants and boots. A black bandanna tied like a headband kept sweat and his spiky brown hair out of his eyes.

There was something wrong with the road up ahead. Something unusually wrong.

It was the way the cracks in it looked. Something screwy about their pattern . . .

The asphalt highway was coated with dust from the yellowish, almost featureless desert to either side. But you could see the shape the road was in, through the dust, and Traveler had learned to read it like a tropics-dweller reading the sky for signs of a monsoon, or a riverboater who watches the currents, who knows instinctively when the river is about to become dangerous.

The road was Traveler's home, his world, his medium. And it was trying to warn him.

Those cracks were new and converging toward the center of the road. As if it had sagged—and then been lifted up again. As if someone had undermined the road and then reinforced it from beneath.

He pumped a round into the chamber of the shotgun in his hands.

He could feel the gun metal warming in the sunlight. It was as if the shotgun were coming to life.

The heavy pump gun was loaded with double-ought buckshot. There was room for eight shells in the tube, but Traveler had only six left. Ammo was hard to come by in post-holocaust America. So hard to come by, it was used as an important trading currency. Traveler had a pretty good supply of ammo for his other guns—there was the AR15 in the weapons rack inside. The two convergently trained 7.62mm HK-21 machine guns mounted to the roof of the van were operated from within the cab by a push button he'd set up on his steering column. There was also a fully loaded Colt .45 Mark IV pistol he carried as a backup in the holster under his jacket.

He scanned the flat horizon. Here and there it was broken by a twisted tree or an outcropping of rock. There was no movement.

But he could sense a trap.

He could feel them, nearby. Something malevolent, and angry, and crippled-up inside. The neurotoxin damage he'd sustained because of Vallone's treachery in that El Hiaguran jungle clearing had had an unforeseen side effect.

7

It had made his senses, at times, almost supernaturally sharp. And it had awakened the animal's sixth sense, present in primeval man but long buried in most modern men—the proximity sense. The sense that feels another Life Energy, nearby.

And now he sensed something—no, someone—beneath him.

"Shit," he muttered, getting back into the van. He tossed the shotgun into the passenger seat, threw the idling vehicle into gear, and backed up, fast.

A quick twenty-five feet, and he stopped the van and stared at the road.

It was buckling, falling like stretched dough, as someone beneath removed support beams. Ten, fifteen, twenty feet. Gone, a pit now. He'd pulled up before, right on the edge of it.

The smart thing to do would be to U-turn, go back, find another route. But it was a hundred miles back to the nearest alternate road. And he had business up ahead. Somewhere farther south was the underground military base occupied by what shreds remained of the U.S. Government. And somewhere in that hidden complex was Major Vallone.

Traveler wanted to have a few words with Vallone.

So he had to go on.

He swung right, into the desert, trying to cut across the wastelands, circle the ambush site, get back on the road.

But they were here, too. There was a screen of waist-high boulders to his right; a flanking team of the ambushers had been waiting there, flattened, expecting him to make just this maneuver.

They leaped up now, and he had a blurry impression of them coming at him. He almost gagged.

They were mutants—what roadrats called Bloats. Swollen, misshapen bodies as distorted as shapes seen in funhouse mirrors, most of them some seven feet tall. Theoretically they were children—none older than fourteen. Children by human standards. But they weren't human. Like some deranged species of ape, they came to full maturity at nine years old. It was the extra holes in their heads that made them hard to look at—inch-wide holes like pointless nostrils scattered about the skull, each of the dozen holes always bubbling with pus and froth or flickering with tiny little pink tongues. Their mouths were so wide they looked as if they went nearly all the way around with just a couple of inches unbroken at the back of the neck. Their eyes drooped unevenly, yellow-filmed and owl-round. Their hands were big as shovels and equipped with long, horny fingers, each one wickedly taloned. They were cunning, and industrious when they wanted to be. And they were always hungry, and human flesh was the most easy prey for them.

They came at him with mouths open so wide he thought their heads would fall apart, big gray tongues vibrating as they yowled out their war cry, which sounded eerily like the air-raid sirens he'd heard just before the bombs came, fifteen years before. They were wearing nothing at all, their scarred, hairy hides hanging in folds over flapping genitals. Each one was carrying a club or a kind of home-made scythe constructed from jagged pieces of scrap metal lashed to splintery wood with strips of leather. One of these swished through his open-side window and slashed at his left shoulder, raking the flesh just enough to leave an arc of blood. Steering with his left hand, he drew the .45 and fired it point-blank into the face of the Bloat angling the crude scythe for another slash. Its lump of a forehead exploded with red, and there was a thirteenth unnatural hole in its head. This one spewed brains as it fell back, sirening plaintively.

Traveler cut to the left, fishtailing over the sand, the

9

four-wheel-drive Meat Wagon spitting grit in spumes behind its massive black wheels as it fought for ground. A dozen mutants clung to it, holding on to the roof, the door handles, the wedgelike snout up front, clawing at the windows, hacking and banging so that metal rang on metal and sparks flew.

He caught a whipping motion out of the corner of his eye and turned in time to see a ten-foot catapult snapping up to lob a bushel-size boulder at him. The big yellow-gray boulder grew, seeming to come on in slow motion.

And then it struck the Meat Wagon's front end. The whole structure shuddered, and the van jounced on its shocks and ground to a halt.

The boulder had broken something in the engine.

Traveler lost his temper.

It wasn't so much that he was probably going to get himself snuffed now, and eaten raw by this walking debris. It was that *they'd screwed up his van*!

He shot a hole through the twisted wrist of a scaly hand reaching through the window; fragments of bone flew, blood spattered, and the thing squealed and jerked its useless hand back. At the same moment Traveler caught up the shotgun and fired it through the right-hand window, catching two Bloats in their stumpy yellow teeth. Gunsmoke filled the cab of the Meat Wagon as he pumped another round into the chamber and let go another ear-splitting shotgun roar through the left-hand window, at a range of one yard, taking a Bloat's head cleanly off its shoulders. The headless body staggered around, clawing at the air, an ugly meat-fountain of blood—and then fell away to be replaced by half a dozen whole Bloats sirening their battle cry.

Traveler pumped his last round into the chamber, raised it to his shoulder, and squeezed the trigger. It was a hard position to be shooting from, the kick from the big shotgun jerking his shoulder unmercifully. The oncoming Bloats were about twenty feet away, whirling the scythes over their hideous heads. They looked like figures of candle wax that had been held too close to the flame. They shrieked as the spreading shotgun pellets lashed into them, putting out eyes and punching into throats.

He tossed the shotgun aside; up ahead the contingent that had been hiding in some side trench under the road had come out, were running at him in a squalid group of eight. He smiled as they came within the convergent-fire scope of his overhead MGs. He pressed the fire button on the steering column.

Nothing happened.

The boulder had knocked out the van's electrical system, which controlled the machine guns.

He scrambled into the back, reaching for the AR15. He heard a scream of pain to his left as a Bloat opened the van's rear door. Traveler had booby-trapped the door, using a spring-tension launcher, and the mutant staggered back with a ten-inch wooden spike through its blood-spurting throat.

Traveler had just gotten the AR15 down, primed and ready, when the next mutie came through the now-unprotected rear door. He swung the rifle around and greeted his unwanted guest with a four-round burst that opened him up like a can of tomato soup. Another one—

But there were two more scrambling through the front.

He squeezed off two shots at the rear door, swung around, and had just time enough to squeeze the trigger once before the stone ax caught him on the side of the head and exploded the world into blue sparkle.

As he sank into unconsciousness, not expecting to wake again, he grasped at one last satisfaction: The son of a bitch who'd clubbed him was going down, too, with a bullet between his animal eyes.

*       *       *

To Traveler's surprise, he woke up.

He seemed to be standing, which didn't make much sense. No, no, he was *dangling,* hanging from his wrists, from the limb of a gnarled tree. Someone else was hanging beside him. A man with a grizzled red face and pain-burned eyes. Up ahead, the Bloats squatted around a camp fire, grunting at one another. Their lower jaws flapped up and down like the lids of inverted pedal-operated trash cans. They were gnawing at something, too, some of them.

A third man hung by his wrists from the tree, on the other side of the tree trunk from Traveler. Traveler's head throbbed; dried blood was caked on his left temple and cheek. His wrists felt like they'd been cut through—he couldn't feel his hands at all. He looked up at the rope binding him to the four-inch-thick branch. It was three-quarter-inch rope, scavenged from some ruin, and rather rotten. He just might be able to chew through it. He took a deep breath and did a pull-up.

The pain brought on by the movement made him grit his teeth to keep from yelling. His arms shuddered as he pulled up, bit by bit, and fresh blood broke out from his head wound to drip warm onto his shoulder. He reached the knot at his wrists—they were bound close together—and began to chew at it. He could feel the tiny strands parting, one by one, but the strain was terrific. His muscles were on fire, and they quivered in protest. The pain in his wrists redoubled and he felt his gorge rising. He was almost relieved when the man beside him whispered hoarsely, "The Bloats are coming."

Traveler let himself sag down to dangle at the end of his arms again, and tried to look oblivious.

The Bloat climbed onto a pile of scree at the foot of the tree trunk and, his head at about the level of Traveler's

12

navel, reached up and clawed away Traveler's jacket and shirt. Then he poked at the bare skin beneath. Traveler winced when the Bloat grabbed a handful of gut muscle and tweaked it hard, apparently to see how much meat was on the prisoner's bones. The Bloat stank like a burst pustule on a corpse. The top of its head showed eight holes, like the holes in one of those bowling balls used only for testing thumb size, and from each one a little pink tongue leaped and waggled, as if eager to taste him. Traveler gagged and looked away.

The Bloat turned away from Traveler and moved to the groaning man on the other side of the tree trunk.

The Bloat took out a long knife and, holding the dangling man pinioned between arm and rib cage, slashed off a hunk of thigh, which it thrust into its mouth. The man screamed piteously and writhed, trying weakly to jerk away. The Bloat held on like a cowboy with a recalcitrant heifer and slashed off another chunk of meat. This one it ran over its hairless head, as if sponging it with the blood—and Traveler realized it was giving all those horrible little pink tongues a taste.

Another Bloat arrived and began to help the first carve the man up more systematically.

After a while the screaming stopped, and there was only the sound of blood dripping and Bloats chewing and the occasionally throaty grunt.

The man dangling beside Traveler sobbed and said, "We'll be next. They'll have us, too, before morning."

# 2

## *The Survivalists*

When the Bloats got tired of stripping the body of the man on the other side of the tree, they returned to the fire, carrying hunks of bloody, steaming man-meat for the others. There were about twenty of them squatting in the ring of yellow firelight. Two or three were smaller, perhaps Bloat children. And there was one immensely fat Bloat, lying on her side: the tribe's Mother, her enormous misshapen breasts like great gunnysacks of lard, dripped over with blood as lesser Bloats hand-fed her.

The corpse hanging on the other side of the trunk was completely intact from the waist up. From the waist down it had been whittled literally to the bone, skeleton legs gleaming pink-white in the distant glow from the fire.

Beyond the slowly swinging, mutilated corpse, Traveler could see the dark hulk of his van. How had they gotten it here? Had they pulled it from the highway?

He looked at the man beside him. "How long you been here?" Traveler asked.

The man's lips moved soundlessly for a few moments before he found the strength to answer. "Maybe—a day. Dunno. Came with three others. I'm the last. We . . . got us a colony. Survivalists. Up in the hills. Near Tahoe. We were bringing in supplies. They just pulled our horses out

14

from under us. Broke the horses' necks. They're . . . punishment . . . Bloats are punishment sent by God because of . . . what we did to the Earth. . . .''

If Traveler hadn't been dangling by his wrists he might've shrugged.

Instead, he did another pull-up and began to gnaw at the rope again.

He'd gotten one hand nearly free when he heard a snarling sound and looked down to see a Bloat emerging from the darkness to his right. Some kind of sentry. Its yellow eyes were on him. Its mouth, like the mouth of a cow, slathering, gray tongue whipping inside as it sirened a warning with ear-raping volume.

At the same moment it scrambled up the scree at him, raising a scythe over its head and swinging it down hard at Traveler's groin.

Traveler kicked out and caught the scythe in the shaft, deflecting it with a steel-toed boot. The Bloat kept coming—and Traveler locked his thighs around the mutant's throat, despite his disgust, and scissored its windpipe with all the strength of his legs. The Bloat dropped the scythe and clawed at his thighs, slobbering septic froth onto his fatigues. It gasped, choking, and flung itself backward, off the mound of rock.

Traveler held fast. The combined weight of the immense Bloat and the two men cracked the tree limb. It snapped off with a loud report, and they fell heavily to the rock. Jagged stones dug into his back, and the Bloat gnashed at his legs.

Traveler's right hand had come loose, and he used it to snatch up the scythe. He drove the long, wickedly curved blade into the mutant's eye and then jerked back on the shaft so the point of the blade popped out the other eye from within. The Bloat's blood spattered thickly, and the thing gave a long, shuddering wail.

15

It thrashed in its death throes as the other Bloats ran up from the camp fire, sirening and swinging clubs.

Traveler worked to free his other hand. But his right worked only clumsily, not yet restored to the efficiency of full circulation.

The three Bloats in the lead were scrambing up the short slope, silhouetted against the firelight, mythic trolls come to life, when a burst of gunshots sent them staggering into one another, clawing at the air as if to punish it for the mysterious attack that seemed to come from nowhere. They fell—and the others stopped, looking around, grunting in confusion.

Traveler broke loose from the limb, cut his companion free, and then ran toward his van. He heard more gunshots and glimpsed the darkened shapes of men running toward the firelight, guns in hand, about thirty feet to his left.

There was a Bloat guarding the van, stumping up and down in front of it, scythe in hand, wondering at all the commotion near the fire. Traveler ducked behind a boulder, then risked a look. The Bloat hadn't seen him. It was staring toward the camp fire, sirening interrogatively. He cut around to its left, moved soundlessly up behind it, and dashed its brains out with a rock.

Adrenaline was carrying him now, adrenaline fueled by rage. Traveler was truly pissed off.

He climbed into the van; the AR15 was where he'd dropped it. They hadn't yet gotten around to scavenging through his stuff. That was lucky. That meant the serum in the van's cooler was okay. The serum that controlled the nerve damage from the neurotoxin . . .

He put a fresh clip into the rifle and climbed out. There was a huge living shape hulking in the darkness. He smelled it and sensed it before he actually saw it. It was at least twelve feet high, heavy as a pilot whale, and smelling

16

like a pilot whale that had been beached a month. It? She. He saw her blocking out the starlight above him, something upraised in her hands. It was the axle of a car, which she swung at him like a club.

"Holy shit!" Traveler burst out, ducking.

Several hundred pounds of metal whistled by close over his head.

The Mother Bloat sirened, her saucerlike yellow eyes fixed on him. She took a step nearer. Her great breasts hung over him, dripping blood and toxic sweat like a couple of bombs about to hit their target.

She raised the axle again and came closer, trapping him against the rear of the van. He popped the rifle to his shoulder and squeezed the trigger three times for three short bursts into her groin, her sternum, and into those dripping yellow eyes.

She let out a bellow, and he had to throw himself aside to avoid the axle dropping from her hands. It struck the gravel to his left with a loud clang.

She staggered back—and then steadied herself. She came at him again, hands outstretched, stumbling.

Christ, Traveler thought. What if she falls on me?

She fell.

He threw himself down and rolled under the van. The huge, blubbery mutant's body hit the gravel with a sickening thud-squish. She flopped about for a few minutes, then lay still. Stinking, oozing, and bleeding.

He realized that he'd dropped the rifle in his hurry to get out from under her. He climbed out from under the van, and, to his disgust, saw that she'd fallen on it. It took him ten minutes to get it free of her—he had to use a small log as a lever to lift her off it.

He carried it wrapped in a rag to the van, and cleaned it off with the kerosene he was currently using as fuel. The van's Wankel rotary would run on almost anything that burned, even perfume.

He heard a noise behind him, at the front door of the van.

He spun, the rifle leveled, and then hesitated.

A man stood there with a guttering torch in his hand, looking at him with grim appraisal. The stranger wore an old, battered U.S. Army ski patroljacket and a GI surplus helmet.

"You're the one cut Jake loose," the man said. "That right?"

"Yeah," Traveler said, lowering his gun, "if Jake was the one hanging from the tree with me. I thought it was kind of rude of him, hanging from my tree and not introducing himself."

He'd lowered the gun, because the other man had his rifle lowered, but he didn't put it aside. He didn't trust the stranger, any more than the stranger trusted him.

"I'm Kettering," the man said. He had longish white hair and white stubble on his drooping face. The flickering torch beside his head made him look cadaverous somehow.

"I'm Traveler."

Kettering nodded. "I thought I recognized the van. Heard about it. Come on out. We'll talk."

He backed up. Traveler climbed over the seats. He had the gun raised now, just to be ready, and as a warning.

Outside, the two men faced one another, looking each other over. A few more gunshots came from the direction of the camp fire.

"You get them all?" Traveler asked.

"I think so. But there's more, out in the desert. They breed and they breed, those vermin. Sometimes we try to find where they keep their tribemothers. Those Mothers'll have four Bloats at a time, like a litter of puppies. Best thing is to find them and kill them."

18

Traveler nodded. "Yeah. For their sakes. I don't think they much like being alive."

He looked up as four men walked up, carrying rifles. Two more were coming along behind, carrying Jake between them.

"How'd you find Jake here?" Traveler asked.

Kettering slung his rifle over his shoulder. "When they didn't come back from the supplies raid, we went out looking. Picked up their trail. Found the dead horses. Followed 'em here. Caught the damned Bloats by surprise."

Traveler nodded—and that hurt. The adrenaline had burned out, and he was feeling like an empty shell, now—empty except for a lot of aches and throbs. His head felt like it was going to split open.

He forced himself to think about his next step.

The Meat Wagon. See if it could be fixed.

"Can I borrow that torch of yours?" he asked. Kettering nodded. Traveler took the torch and carried it to the engine compartment, looking inside. The boulder had dented the fender pretty badly and maybe put the front end a little out of alignment. But he couldn't see anything wrong with the engine.

"There," Kettering said, looking over his shoulder. "Them wires there. See 'em? On the distributor?" He reached past Traveler and hooked the wires up again.

Traveler passed him the torch and got into the van, twisted the key in the ignition. He breathed a long sigh of relief as the engine turned over and purred. The Meat Wagon was all he had. It was the axis of his world. It kept him moving, going places. The world was tolerable only when you kept *moving* through it. The movement created the illusion that there just might be something better over the next rise. Although he knew that what he was more likely to find over the next rise was more desolation, radioactive hotspots, burned-out cities and burned-out minds and burned-out souls. Ashes.

But if you kept moving, you could tell yourself that you were leaving that place behind.

That van was almost everything to him.

And, goddamn it, parts were hard as fucking hell to get now.

He reached out, and slammed the van door. "I'll be going now," he said. It couldn't be far back to the highway. He still had one intact headlight.

A man with an Air Force cap and a blue flight jacket walked up to Kettering, an M16 held white-knuckled in his hands. "You ain't gonna let him go like that, are you?"

Kettering cocked his head to one side. He seemed to be considering.

Traveler found the .45 on the seat beside him. He held it ready. The rifle was propped up next to him. He waited. He didn't want just to back the van out; if they started shooting they might knock out his tires. Tires were hard to come by, too. He only had one spare.

He knew what the man in the blue flight jacket meant. The Meat Wagon itself would be a treasure to these people. Top-quality operational vehicles were few and far between. These people had probably come here from their settlement on horses. Maybe they'd already decided they'd like to use the van for a tractor. And the weapons on it were worth their weight in gold.

Finally, Kettering said, "He cut Jake loose. He didn't have to do that. He mighta run and left Jake for them vermin. Jake's my son. We owe him one, this Traveler. Anyway, maybe we could hire him to—"

Traveler put the van in gear, began slowly moving ahead, looking for a place to turn around. He felt sick and dizzy. He needed sleep. But first he had to get away from here.

The man in the flight jacket pointed his M16 through the side window of the van. "Stop that van and get out," he said.

# 3

## The Job

The muzzle of the M16 was about eight inches from Traveler's heart.

So he stopped the van.

"You're making my headache worse," Traveler said in a dangerously reasonable voice. "That's not a wise move."

The man in the flight jacket was gaunt and shaggy. He wore glasses with only one lens. He kept the eye shut, under the part of the frame where the lens was missing. His other eye was open and defiantly cocked at Traveler. "Don't you try nothin'. We got to talk. We need you bad, see. We got to talk."

Kettering pressed the man aside. The M16 withdrew. Kettering leaned against the door on an elbow, casually, as one country farmer talking to another. The torch guttered in his other hand. "We've had a colony, see, up in the hills, from *before* the Big Drop. We knew it was coming."

"Survivalists," Traveler said.

Kettering nodded. "And we done okay. Till lately. Started getting some bad harassment from roadrats and other such scum. Guerrilla raiders. Communists, they are. Now, what we figure to do, is hold on and keep putting it all back together, and in maybe in a generation or three we'll have the United States going again like it used to be.

Or like it could go in that direction. But these here communists, they're raiding our women, our horses, our fuel. . . . We need to hit 'em back, see. Get some of our stuff back. And we could sure use your help. A killing machine like this . . .'' He patted the metal of the Meat Wagon's flank. ''And a fella like you. I heard about you. You were the one that cut the Black Rider's army right in two. I heard you was the most dangerous man on the roads. But they say you give a damn about people, too—''

''They were wrong about that part.''

Kettering grinned, showing blackened teeth.

''I'm not so sure about that. But I don't rightly care—I plan to pay you to do the work. We ain't asking for charity. We can offer you a tank of gas. A woman. Why, you could have a night or two with all our women—we need some new breedin' blood in the camp. And ammo. What you say? They say you take on jobs. Well, I'm offering you a job.''

Traveler sighed. But it was true he was running short on ammo and fuel.

''Tell you what. We head out, you come along behind on your horses. We make camp and talk about it tomorrow.''

''You got yourself a deal. But—drive slowly. *Real* slowly.''

''I wasn't going to run out on you,'' Traveler said wearily. ''Get your horses and let's get the hell out of here.''

The headache that woke him the next morning was to be his constant companion for the next two days.

His toxin-damaged nerves were humming, and every sound, no matter how slight, came at him like a pistol shot beside his ear. He put his hands over his ears and sat up on the narrow cot, wincing. He just might have a concussion from that cudgel stroke. No use worrying about it. Doctors

23

and hospitals were a thing of the past. Witch doctors were making a big comeback.

He fumbled open the door of the minifridge behind the passeger seat, found a vial of antitoxin, uncorked it, and drank half of it off. How many vials left? he wondered as the toxin cooled his system, eased the throbbing, lowered the volume in his ears. Maybe fifty. He had the formula— but to find a place that could synthesize it . . .

It wasn't impossible. But it was close to it.

Traveler replaced the vial and thought about the men who'd been on that special mission in El Hiagura when the neurotoxin had been sprayed on them from the copters. Hill, Orwell, and Margolin. Vallone had told them that there would be no El Hiaguran government forces in the jungle; he sent them into that zone knowing the neurotoxin weapon was being tested there. And the men that had been with Traveler had never gotten the antitoxin Traveler had lucked into. . . . Someday, maybe, he'd find them. If they were still alive. And if they hadn't gone mad yet.

Breakfast was a tin of sardines and a hunk of moldy bread. A cup of water. Then he went out to check on the Survivalists.

Dawn was an hour worn away. They were camped atop a low hill, in a ring of boulders. The men who'd stood watch during the night sat around the fire, drinking highly caffeinated ersatz coffee—probably they'd traded to the Army for it—and yawning. They wore bits and pieces of military clothing. Each one carried a canteen and a mess kit, survivalist paraphernalia purchased before the war. To one side was a tumbledown shack; from beneath a yarrow-stick jumble of boards a skeletal arm was extended, bleached white. A skull glowered emptily from a hummock of scrub.

The sky was slate-colored; the desert below the hill was

banded with brown and yellow, studded with boulders and etched with dry washes.

Traveler accepted a cup of the acrid coffee and sat down on a low boulder a little apart from the others, pretending to sip. He didn't drink coffee—he couldn't handle stimulants. His nerves were hyperpitched already. He'd taken it as a gesture of camaraderie. It was better than having to make conversation.

He needed the job, but he was reluctant to accept it. He was uncomfortable around people, especially when there were more than one or two. And he knew that sooner or later they'd ask him to confirm the stories. Already the younger ones were watching him sidelong, working up their nerve to ask if it was true that he'd done this, that he'd done that . . .

It was a pain in the ass.

Kettering came into camp after having relieved himself in the bushes. He shuffled up to Traveler, M16 crooked in his arm. Probably he slept with it.

He sat down on a rock beside Traveler. "I've been thinking about my daughter Junie," he said. "She's got the prettiest damn red hair. I think you'd like her. I'd like to see her have a kid—even if you had to move on afterward. The colony's population is down. I had another daughter, but the roadrats got her. Found her body later and wished I hadn't. Anyway, Junie, now, I think she'd—"

Traveler was annoyed. "You hiring me to fight these communist guerrillas you told me about or to be a breeding stud? That's two different jobs. Needs two different salaries."

"Them girls is salary enough. But we're offering you ammo and food and fuel to help us out with the guerrillas."

"Where'd you get your supplies? Like this coffee?"

"The army runs a trading depot over in Drift."

"The Glory Boys?"

25

"They guard it. But it's some army storekeeper we deal with . . . I don't know why they pretend they're the 'U.S.' Army. They ain't nothing like it. That government is dead as a squashed bug. Whatever this thing is they got in Vegas, it ain't the U.S. Government."

President Frayling had survived the War—he'd been up in Air Force One at the time—and had established a base in Nevada, in an underground NORAD installation near Las Vegas. He had fantasies of restoring the power of the U.S.A. with force of arms. He had perhaps a thousand soldiers left, and a picked fighting elite of biker-warriors called The Glory Boys. To keep his installation functioning he and his administrators dealt in food goods—they had a vast underground store of reserves—in exchange for "draftees," which meant slaves; and weapons or valuable metals. Vallone was somewhere in that installation. . . .

"So what do you say, Traveler?" Kettering asked.

"I'll take the job on one condition. I've got to be left to myself. I camp by myself. If I want women I'll go looking for them. I don't want them brought to me."

"Sure, sure, whatever you say." He got up. "I'm going to have a look at the horses, get 'em packed up and watered. We'll be ready to move out at oh-seven-thirty."

The Survivalists' encampment was a depressing broken-down collection of Quonset huts half-buried under humps of earth; there were reeking outhouses, salvaged junk of every kind cluttering up the yards, and feral, suspicious-eyed people stood listlessly about. The whole squalid stew was surrounded by a tangled barbed-wire fence and a wooden spike-topped barricade. A red-haired girl watched him drive by. Junie.

Kettering's "pretty red-haired Junie" was a sallow, horsey-faced girl with matted red hair. She wore clodhopper shoes and overalls.

Traveler drove the Meat Wagon through the camp, the van bouncing and swaying as it negotiated the deeply rutted dirt road. He parked the van near an old leaning barn, the sole remains of a farm that had once stood here. He got out of the van and looked around. There was a pile of horse manure behind the barn, adding its smell to the numerous foul odors of the place. He could hear horses stamping and shifting in the mossy-sided barn.

To one side stood a battered Chevrolet station wagon, stripped of its chrome and fenders, its sides crudely armored with strapped-on sheet metal.

Kettering and his men led the horses into the barn. Several women, each of them less attractive than Junie, gathered in a clutch around the chief's daughter to whisper and titter as they stared at Traveler. He pretended to study the terrain around the camp, not wanting to encourage them with so much as a glance.

The camp was on the flattened top of a ridge at the foot of the Sierras. The mountains bulked purple and mostly barren above them, patched with the green fur of pines and desert trees. Lake Tahoe was on the other side of those mountains. It was said that a Soviet ICBM had struck near the lake, obliterating Reno—and the military base nearby— and rendering the area unlivable, a radioactive hotspot. But something lived there—something hideously mutated lived in that lake and crawled out now and then, leaving eight-foot-wide slimy traces behind it. No one had ever seen it—no one who survived to describe it.

Some of the colonizers bore the marks of radiation sickness—they'd survived the fallout but had been marked by it. There were a number of malformed children. But none of them were severely retarded or so badly malformed they couldn't work. Radiation victims of that kind— "doomed in the womb," they were called—were put to death. The survivors had to be practical.

27

Kettering came out of the barn, four young men following him. "These here, Traveler, are Morris and Burt," indicating two tall, gawky, black-haired brothers. "And this is Harry." A stocky, squint-eyed man wearing a dusty white cowboy hat. "And this here is Joe." A jock-sized guy with a ragged crewcut and a permanent sneer. All four wore fatigues, as if they represented a kind of special militia in the colony. "They're our Security Team," Kettering said. "They're gonna be your special assistants. They're good fighting men."

Traveler looked them over dubiously. Good fighting men?

Morris and Burt each had an M16. The short dumpy one, Harry, had a revolver strapped around his middle gunfighter-style, and Joe had what looked like a 30.06 deer rifle with a scope on it. The scope, however, was bent. He saw Traveler looking at that. "Gonna fix that," Joe said.

Kettering moved closer to Traveler. Traveler took a step back.

"Didja see that redhead?" Kettering asked in a stage whisper. "That's my Junie."

The girls tittered.

"What'd you think of her?" Kettering asked.

Traveler forced himself to keep his expression neutral. "Ah, I see what you mean."

"Yes, sir. Now if you'd like to—"

He was interrupted by the howl of a siren. "We're under attack!" Morris and Burt shouted simultaneously. They turned and ran into one another, bouncing off to fall on their asses.

Traveler sighed.

He climbed into the van and came out with his Heckler and Koch HK91 heavy assault rifle. The big automatic rifle at port arms, he ran behind Kettering and the four

28

men of the "Security Team" to the front gate. A man in a thirty-foot wooden guard tower was firing at something on the other side of the gate. There was a short burst of return fire, and the guard toppled over backward, falling on his head in the dust of the compound. Other men had taken up defensive stations at firing slits inside the wooden walls. He peered through one of the slits, seeking a target.

It was twilight, hovering on the edge of sunset. The gnarled pines outside the colony compound's perimeters were throwing long shadows across the lichen-splashed humps of boulders strewn randomly over the top of the ridge. He glimpsed men in ragged green-and-brown camouflage fatigues crouching and running from boulder to boulder, tree to tree, coming closer. Not many—maybe ten. But there might be a lot more, somewhere in concealment.

"That's them!" Kettering shouted. "The guerrillas!"

Traveler nodded. The Survivalists were probably being raided for supplies and livestock. Traveler wondered how much Kettering really knew about these people, and why the old man was so sure they were communists. He probably regarded any hostile stranger as a communist.

Traveler shouted, "Hold your fire till they get closer! You're wasting ammo!"

They didn't hear him over the racket. Traveler had to go to them one at a time and shout at them.

Just as the gunfire died down a massive explosion shook the ground. It had come from behind.

"Shit!" Kettering yelled. "There was nobody on the back gate!"

Traveler ran toward the coiling column of smoke rising just beyond the barn, thinking, The attack at the front gate was a decoy.

He was worried. His van was the most valuable item at

29

the back end of the camp. And if he didn't get there in time . . .

He didn't. He got there in time to see that the fence had been blown open in the back, leaving a ten-foot-wide gap. Judging from the color of the smoke, the explosive had been simple construction-site dynamite.

Four men on horseback were driving half a dozen skinny stallions through the gap. Two more ran out of the barn, carrying sacks of feed, pistols in their hands. When they saw Traveler running toward them, they turned and raised their pistols to fire. He had to cut them down, sawing them both through at their middles with one long horizontal burst from the HK91.

They spun, the feed sacks falling; the feed sacks had been shot open, and the grain from one of them was mixing with the blood of the man who'd been carrying it.

Traveler ran past them, sprinting now.

Someone was driving the Meat Wagon out the back gate.

# 4

## *The Pursuit*

Traveler stood staring after the van, watching his life drive away. Even more than the Meat Wagon, he needed the antitoxins in it. Without them, he'd go mad.

The Security Team ran up beside him. "Jeesis Mary and Joseph, they got our horses!" Joe shouted. "They got our horses!"

"Fuck your horses—" Traveler began.

"Kettering won't let us," Morris tried to explain. "He says it's—"

"Never mind!" Traveler shouted. "Just tell me this— does that station wagon work?"

"Station wagon?" Morris wasn't familiar with the term. He looked to Burt for help. His brother gaped back at him.

Traveler pointed at the Chevy.

"Oh!" Burt said, his face lighting up with comprehension. "You mean, The Car! Why sure, that's the camp's car. Sure it works! I got to drive it once!"

"Hey, big deal," Morris said. "You only got to drive it in the compound."

Traveler turned to Joe. "Get some fuel into that car, and any extra cans it'll carry. Also some food and water and ammo."

Joe's eyes widened. "You can't take The Car out of

31

the camp! Kettering won't allow it! It's the only one we got.''

Traveler gritted his teeth. With each passing second The Meat Wagon was getting farther away. "What the hell do you keep it for if you don't take it out? Is it a historical monument or a planter?"

"A what?"

"Never mind. It's there for emergencies, right?"

Joe nodded.

Traveler barked, "Well what the fuck do you think this is? They stole your horses, didn't they? You want your horses back, right? Then we've got to go get them!"

Joe considered this as the Meat Wagon drove farther and farther away.

"We'll have to ask Kettering," he announced. "That's what we'll have to do."

Kettering was just trotting up to them, wheezing. "They—they got the horses?"

Traveler almost said, "Fuck the horses!" again, but he was afraid Kettering would say, "I don't allow it." So instead: "Kettering—you want those horses back? I'll get 'em back for you. Get that car ready to go and give me two of these nitwits to take with me, and I'll see those guerrillas don't bother you again."

Kettering hesitated. The van drove on, and on. Finally, "Okay. But you take all four boys with you."

This was, Traveler knew, not to give him additional firepower against the enemy but to send along insurance that Traveler would bring The Car back.

"Sure, sure."

Kettering went to prepare The Car. The Security Team went with him—except for Joe, who remained, glowering at Traveler, filled with suspicion.

Traveler went to inspect the Chevy. It seemed rugged. The engine was in good shape. But it would run only on gasoline, so he hoped they had plenty of extra.

32

Ten minutes later he was driving the Chevy down a narrow mountain road. One headlight remained on the car. The shocks were shot, and the engine knocked every time he punched the accelerator, but considering that there hadn't been a repair garage open for fifteen years, the car wasn't in bad shape.

Traveler was thinking, Now what?

He had no idea what.

They could be anywhere. Probably the ones with the horses would have cut across the countryside. The guerrillas who'd stolen his car would have to remain more or less on the roads, at least until the country flattened out.

"You got any idea where these people hole up?" he asked Joe, who sat beside him.

"What? Sure! Southeast, in the lava fields!"

Traveler was relieved until Burt chimed in. "Southeast! Bullshit! They moved north up to the flats now!"

"Out southa Drift what I heard," Morris said. "They ain't on the flats no more."

"In other words," Traveler said coldly, "you don't have any idea where they are."

"They're what you call nomadic," Harry said. "Move around a lot."

"I guess that's right," Joe admitted.

Traveler swore softly. This wasn't going to be easy. And these bumpkins were getting on his nerves. The anti-toxin would wear off soon. Already he could feel the presence of the four other men with psychic keenness. They seemed to press claustrophobically in on him. He forced himself to concentrate on driving.

The switchback road followed the rippling contours of the foothills, winding through a rocky pine forest. Now and then a moth flared white in the car's single headlight. A jackrabbit looked at them from the middle of the road, startled, its ears straight up, its eyes glowing pink in the reflected light.

"Rabbit!" Burt hooted. "Let's git it for dinner!"

As if sensing the train of Burt's thoughts, the rabbit bounded into the darkness.

"You couldn't hit the damn thing, anyway, Burt," Joe said, "unless you caught it asleep and stuck the gun in its ear!"

Harry laughed at this. "Burt and Morris don't shoot very straight, but they sure like to shoot *at* things! I remember when we raided that settlement down the mountain and he shot up that schoolhouse, ol' Burt chasin' those kids around. Had to corner one before he could hit him with that rifle."

Traveler looked at Joe. "You guys raid other camps?"

"Huh? Sure. How else we gonna survive?"

Traveler thought, So much for these people representing civilization's last best hope.

"I remember one time," Morris said, "when we burned down that settlement on the flatlands, and that old woman chased Harry with a broom! Boy, you sure looked funny!"

"My gun was jammed," Harry said pettishly. "But I got it unjammed and then I gave her a gutful of .44s—"

"Shut up," Traveler said.

Joe looked at him. "What?"

"You heard me. I said shut up. I don't want to hear any more of this bullshit. I want to concentrate."

He pulled up at the edge of the road where the curve bellied outward to overlook a deep valley. Down below he saw a single headlight faint and far away. It cut behind a curve and was gone.

"That's got to be the guy," Traveler muttered. "This road diverge down below?"

"Nope," Harry said firmly. "It goes on for ten miles or more without hitting another."

Traveler nodded grimly. "Then hold on."

He pulled back into the road and stepped on the gas.

"What you doing!" Joe yelled, gripping the dashboard. "Kettering'll have our hides if we wreck this car!"

"Wreck the car!" Burt cried. "He's gonna get us all killed!"

The station wagon was barreling along the narrow one-lane dirt-and-gravel road at sixty mph. Sixty-five. Seventy . . .

To the left was a sheer drop of about two hundred yards. At the bottom of the drop were boulders and trees.

The car careened around the curves, skating on the gravel, its heavy rear end doing a hip-shimmy, wheels shrieking.

Seventy-five, eighty . . .

The mountain cliff-face to their right whipped by so fast its details were lost. Just a blur. Joe and Burt and Morris and Harry hung on, swearing when the inertia threatened to wrench them loose.

"Joe, goddamnit, take the wheel away from him!" Harry shouted from the rear.

"Try it," Traveler said over the roar of the engine, "and I'll stuff that toy gun of yours up your ass till it comes out your mouth."

Joe just hung on and shut his eyes.

The car shrieked down the steep road, and at the next switchback nearly went off into the void—it tilted up on two wheels and slid sideways as Traveler fought to keep it on the road. And then they were around, and it banged down on all four wheels again, bouncing along the straightaway.

The wind screamed past the windshield. The world spun crazily with each turn. Traveler's pulse outraced the engine's pistons.

Get that son of a bitch, he thought. Catch him. Get him.

35

His fingers were white on the wheel, his mouth was grim. He was shaking with rage. Joe, considering trying to take over, turned to look at him—and then shrank back.

Harry yelled, "All right, I've had it!" as the car nearly went over the cliff edge a second time. He drew his gun and pressed it to the back of Traveler's head. "Slow down or I blow you away!"

Traveler just smiled.

At this speed, if Harry killed him the car would go out of control for sure. Harry'd be killing himself, too.

Of course, Harry and the others were amazingly stupid. They just might be stupid enough to do it.

But he held on to the wheel, smiling coldly, playing Russian roulette with Harry's panic and brainpower.

After a moment, Harry sat back, cursing.

Five minutes later the road bottomed out, and they were bouncing through a pine forest on a relatively straight road. Up ahead, Traveler could make out the flicker of the Meat Wagon's headlight.

"You son of a bitch, how dare you touch my car!" he said between grinding teeth.

He pressed the accelerator to the floor, and the station wagon, protesting, leapt ahead. The engine whined; he could hear the knock. He was afraid it wasn't going to make it. The Car just might break down from the stress. The Meat Wagon, on the other hand, was tuned and recently rebuilt—he'd taken advantage of his chance to do that in Kansas City. And it had the edge on the Chevy in terms of sheer horsepower.

When the guerrilla who'd stolen the van realized he was being tailed, he'd step on it and leave them behind.

There was nothing to do but keep doggedly on.

Traveler slowed as the dirt road jogged into a cracked asphalt highway, heading south. He drove on through the night, managing to keep up with the Meat Wagon without

36

gaining on it. He deliberately held back; if he tried to overtake the van now he'd lose it. His only hope was to hold back, like he was just another vagabond, and wait for the van to pull over, maybe at some trading station or water supply, or just to take a piss. Then he'd have the bastard.

As the night wore on, some of his anger wore off, and he began to realize that what the guy who'd stolen his van had done was only what he'd have done himself. Probably the guy was part of one of the bands of people who'd fallen together for survival, helter-skelter, trying to keep alive, faced with famine, exposure, fuel shortage, bad water, no doctors, no medicines, no police to call when the roadrats came at you. The whole world an enemy. And whoever it was, they'd acted bravely. They hadn't done any gratuitous killing at the colony, as Harry and Burt and the others bragged of having done elsewhere. They did only what was necessary.

Yeah, Traveler had to grudgingly understand and respect them.

But, by God, he was going to stop the guy, too.

The night wore on, and wore out Harry and Joe and Burt and Morris. They snored in their seats. Traveler knew that both he and the guy who'd hijacked his van were taking a big chance, barreling along like this in the darkness. The roadrats had a way of setting night-traps. Hard to see on an unlit road with just one headlight. And then, too, the road might suddenly end. . . .

As he thought that, something black-gray loomed up, filling the road. He nearly piled into an overturned school bus.

He whipped around it, shooting off the road, bumping through the flat, featureless desert that now surrounded them, then back onto the highway again on the other side of the bus, the whole maneuver taking three seconds. He'd had a glimpse of small skeletons in the school bus. Bleaching there for fifteen years. He glanced at his dashboard Geiger counter. Reading normal.

He'd been feeling sleepy, before the bus had loomed up. The near crash had charged him up with adrenaline. He was thoroughly awake now.

But at dawn he was sagging in his seat.

"Where the hell are we?" Joe asked, stretching.

"You tell me," Traveler said.

"The flatlands," Harry said, waking up in the back. "Looks like the territory north of Drift. Maybe five miles out."

The desert sky was becoming pale gunmetal. There was enough light to make out the Meat Wagon, a notch on the horizon up ahead. Traveler glanced at the gas meter. "Low on fuel . . ."

And then the Meat Wagon was nearer, nearer. Had it stopped?

It had slowed. Because there was a roadrat barrier across the road, and roadrats were closing in on both vehicles, from both sides, guns blazing.

# 5

## The Good, the Bad . . .

Three cars and a three-wheeled motorcycle. The cars hardly looked like cars anymore. They looked like some kind of spiky sea animal on wheels. They were covered with spikes and roll bars and gun snouts. On the nearest, some kind of low-slung sedan, a row of withered human heads hung on a line between two poles, dead hair streaming in the wind as the car came on. The grill had been removed, and in its place was a ramming wedge of welded steel. On the top face of the wedge they'd painted a gaping mouth full of jagged teeth.

Now he could see the roadrats in the car on the left, a stripped-down convertible whose sides were tricked out with eight-inch serrated teeth. The roadrats inside—six of them crowded in—wore ragtag leather and animal hides; some of them had hubcaps strapped to their arms like shields. Their faces were painted and their eyes bright with flash-weed and booze. They came on war-whooping and waving their crossbows, their guns and their knife-tipped cudgels. The dawn light seemed to flare up as they came, showing them in greater detail. On his left a triple-mohawked roadrat stood in the front passenger seat of the convertible, pointing a pistol over the top of the windshield, grinning. He wore a woman's long blue coat, and there were brassieres tied around his biceps like armbands of some secret society. Bandoliers crosscrossed his chest—but instead of bullets they contained dried human fingers. He wore crudely tanned pants of Negro hide—a prized favorite among the more racist roadrat troupes—with steel spikes on pads crowning knees and shins. He was a classic roadrat, and there was something almost aristocratic in the hodgepodge styling of his outrage-gear.

Traveler put a .45 bullet through his head, just below the center mohawk.

Firing across his body with his right hand, steering with his left, Traveler zigzagged down the road as bullets zinged off the station wagon's crude armoring and webbed the rear window with cracks.

The roadrats were moving parallel to the station wagon now, trying to hem it in. Just up ahead was the roadblock. One of the roadrats standing in the back of the speeding convertible raised a homemade crossbow and fired a bolt that was caught by the wind of the car's passage and deflected directly through the rear side window of the station wagon. He had calculated it nicely—the bolt sank to its quivering fletch in Burt's chest. Burt died, whimpering, as his brother clutched at him.

Harry was taking potshots out the window, with no good effect. Joe fired a more useful M16 burst out the right window. Two roadrats slumped in their seats, blood caught in the wind and spraying along behind them. The barrier loomed up ahead.

Behind, the three-wheeled motorcycle, a trike, was coming up close as its driver angled to fire a crude marlin-spike launcher mounted on his handlebars through the rear window. He fired, there was a thunk sound, and Morris was impaled, pinned to the back of Joe's seat, quivering and instantly dead.

The roadblock was just twenty feet ahead when Traveler hit the brakes hard.

The trike, as Traveler had anticipated, ran into the rear of the station wagon, and the rider screamed as he was pitched into the rear window, which had been already partly broken by the marlin-spike and bullets. He hung half in, half out of the window, his neck broken, the bike a crumpled ruin on the roadside, as Traveler backed around it, angling between two roadrat cars.

He backed onto the desert sands, snugging the station wagon's rear against a boulder—smashing the dangling roadrat corpse in the rear window against the rock—and fired twice more out the side window at two roadrats running up from the stopped convertible, one with a rifle in his hand, the other with a stick of dynamite. Traveler missed the one with the rifle, but one of his slugs exploded the left knee of the roadrat with the dynamite, who was a little ahead of his friend. The dynamite's fuse was lit and sparking as the man fell in his friend's path. The rifle-toting roadrat was pocking the front end of the station wagon with bullet-holes, then he tripped over his friend and fell atop the stick of dynamite. Both of them went up in the explosion, their entrails and blood mixing in a blast-bubble in the air—true friendship.

The driver of the Meat Wagon had executed a beautiful U-turn, was wending between roadrats like a test driver on an obstacle course, firing out the side window now and then with impressive accuracy, using some kind of light hand-pistol—probably some 9mm of one sort or another. With a pistol like that you had to be accurate, and more than one roadrat fell with a bullet in the brain. Traveler was impressed. He wished he could get a look at the guy.

He cursed himself for not having set the booby traps that usually protected the Meat Wagon from hijacking. But the attack siren had distracted him. . . .

Now the Meat Wagon had broken through the screen of roadrats, was doing another U-turn so that once again it faced the roadblock. For a moment it was like a bull checking out the matadors, snorting and pawing.

Meanwhile, Harry and Joe, now both with M16s, were plunking rounds into the convertible. The last roadrat in the convertible fell over dead, and Traveler shouted, "Save your ammo!" He hit the gas and brought the station wagon, jouncing, back onto the road, backed it up so that it was side by side with the Meat Wagon. He couldn't see through the van's armored firing slits. He considered trying to take the Meat Wagon back now, but there was no time; the roadrats were chivvying them again, coming once more from the sides.

The roadrat barrier across the road was flanked on both sides by piled-up boulders and logs—the terrain was impassable for a long way on both sides, with clusters of boulders in the way. They'd have to go through the barrier. It was too thick for one car to ram and get through. But two might do it.

Traveler glanced at the Meat Wagon and saw that the shutter in the side window had been drawn back just enough so that he could see the hijacker's rather skinny hand, signaling to him. The hijacker had had the same thought: He was suggesting they ram the roadblock together. Traveler reached out into the hijacker's line of sight and signaled agreement, just as the two roadrat vehicles came screaming hard at them, firing, cutting in from two sides of the road. Traveler grinned and hit the gas. The Meat Wagon lurched ahead at the same moment, both the van and the station wagon moving out of the intersecting target area of the two oncoming roadrat sedans.

The sedans missed their targets and collided head-on with each other, exploding, an entangling of steel and smashing bodies, a ball of flame around blackening metal seen in Traveler's outside rearview mirror.

The Meat Wagon and the station wagon accelerated and squeezed as close together as they dared—just three inches between them—to concentrate their ramming force.

Traveler felt strange forced into the ironic position of having to collaborate with the guy who'd stolen his car.

The roadblock was forty yards away. Thirty. Twenty-five . . .

It was a hastily cobbled together affair of pine logs and sheet metal and roped-on tires and uprooted tree trunks.

Traveler and the hijacker were taking a big risk: There just might be something else hidden behind the barrier. Maybe a pit. Maybe a boulder.

The two vehicles screamed closer and closer to the barrier. Harry and Joe were shouting at Traveler, "Man, are you crazy? We gonna die! Go back, go back, what the fuck you—"

A glimpse of terrified roadrat faces as the human scum scrambled to get out from behind the barrier. Two of the braver ones remained, raising rifles to get a bead at the oncoming vehicles. Traveler hunched low behind the wheel—a bullet starred the windshield just over his head.

Joe screamed and ducked under the dashboard as—

They impacted.

With a bone-crunching sound the two vehicles rammed into the roadblock, the steel frames of the van and station wagon shuddering, headlights shattering, fragments of wood and human bodies flying.

And then they were through, speeding side by side down the road.

There was a little complication, though, that Traveler didn't know about. He couldn't see the roadrat clinging to the roof rack of the station wagon. At the moment of impact, when the vehicles had been slowed by the barrier, he'd leapt onto the Chevy from a boulder to one side of the barrier. He was inching his way over the roof, toward the driver's side. . . .

Inside the car, Joe was climbing back up onto his seat, muttering, "We—we made it. We got through! Gawd day-em!"

The road ahead was clear and straight, a plumb line through the desert. Somewhere up ahead was the derelict town Drift.

The Meat Wagon was creeping ahead of the station wagon, accelerating to leave it behind.

Traveler knew he didn't have the weight to force the van off the road. And he didn't want to damage it by cutting in front of it, forcing a crash. There was an extra can of fuel in the back of the station wagon—soon he'd have to stop and pour it into the tank. From what he knew of the Meat Wagon's fuel situation, the other driver could go on for at least another ten miles.

Maybe he could trick the guy. . . .

He accelerated to come into the hijacker's line of sight and signaled out the side window, making the hand sign that in New Road Lingo meant "Stop—let's parley. I have something to trade with you."

He caught a glimpse of the hijacker's hand signaling, "Negative."

And then the van surged ahead, pouring on the speed. Maybe the hijacker had recognized the station wagon from the Survivalists' camp. Probably.

Traveler had no choice but to—

A blood-spattered face, upside down, leered at him from the windshield, blocking his view of the road. The roadrat clinging to the roof. The roadrat's face was pressed against the glass, deforming comically. Blood from a head wound trickled down the glass in long, thin red fingers.

Traveler raised his .45 to fire through the glass.

44

At the same moment, the roadrat tossed something precious in through the window. It was something he'd probably carried around for a long time, knowing it was valuable, thinking maybe of trading it for a good rifle. Maybe he'd gotten it off the body of a dead Glory Boy. In the roadrat warrior culture, it was something rare and valuable. It was a hand grenade.

And it was sitting in Traveler's lap, with its pin pulled.

Traveler grabbed it with his left hand—the hand that had been holding the wheel. He had to let the wheel go to do that, but he had no choice. His right hand was encumbered by the pistol. He tossed the grenade out the window a split second before it exploded. It exploded low, near the rear end, and the big car kicked its hind legs, lifting up off the road, coming down with both rear tires shattered, grinding out sparks on its wheel rims. It fishtailed and veered. The roadside sagebrush filled the windshield. The leering face on the glass vanished, the world spun, and the station wagon came to a shuddering stop in the desert grit.

"Shit," Joe said, and that pretty much covered Traveler's feelings in the matter.

Traveler was tired, aching, hungry, and disgusted. There were two corpses in the car with him, and one dangling from the rear window.

And where was the asshole who'd dropped the grenade through the window?

Colt in his hand, he opened the car's door and threw himself out, shoulder-rolling, coming up with the gun at ready.

Nobody on the roof.

He looked around. About ten feet behind the car the roadrat was lying in a crumpled heap, lips moving listlessly. Looked like his back was broken—hit a rock at the wrong angle when he fell off the car.

45

Traveler walked up to him and, avoiding looking in the guy's eyes, put a bullet through his head.

He felt an acrid aftertaste of regret. The guy had been ballsy.

It was easy to hate the roadrats, because it was easy to forget that most of them had once been regular, hardworking American men. Mechanics, truck drivers, high school students, whatever. The war had been too much. Their families had died; their plans, their ambitions, their little dreams. Their world. And they'd had the bad luck to survive. It had been too much for them—and they went mad. Had become drugging, boozing, rapine-hungry savages with their own perverse subculture and tribalism. Each roadrat "outfit" had its own names. They tattooed them onto their chests. This one belonged to the Gutbusters.

The roadrats at the roadblock probably wouldn't follow. They'd be scavenging their own dead, and reluctant to risk it all again so soon.

Traveler returned to the car. Harry and Joe were looking at it, shaking their heads disgustedly.

"The Car," Joe kept saying. "Look at it. The Car."

"Stop whining," Traveler said irritably. He was thinking about the Meat Wagon. It had vanished down the road.

The station wagon was still smoking. As he watched, flames began to lick up from the underside.

"Shit!" Harry bellowed. "Get the gas!"

They risked their lives getting the extra gas can out of the car. It was as valuable as a man's life.

They got the can out, and the food, and had gotten twenty feet away when the car exploded.

Traveler watched it burn with a certain satisfaction. Joe and Harry sobbed.

Traveler forced himself to take it easy for a few minutes, though he wanted to start down the road after the van.

There was some hope he could steal a car in Drift and continue the chase.

But he needed rest and food. They sat down in the shade of a small pine and ate, the three men passing tins of beans and fruit. Traveler dozed for a while.

And then his eyes snapped open.

Harry and Joe were gone. There was a low hill to one side. And from the other side of the hill came gunshots and screams.

# 6

## . . . And the Ugly

Carrying the HK91 assault rifle, Traveler climbed to the top of the hill and looked down at the scene in the little hollow on the other side.

Joe and Harry, M16s in hand, were standing outside a makeshift shack. Three red-spattered bodies lay at their feet. Joe was looking them over like a pawnshop jeweler dubiously assaying the price of a watch. "Ain't got much on 'em," he said, bending to paw through the clothes of the two dead children and the old man.

Traveler felt sick to his stomach. These assholes had stumbled on some little salvager's camp and blown them away for no good reason. Traveler had to repress the impulse to give Joe and Harry the same treatment. But he might need them yet. They could be useful backups. And if he got their damn horses back and took them to their colony, he could get his pay. He hated to leave them alive, though.

He started down the hill.

Joe and Harry looked up and watched him coming without concern. They'd already looted the dead for what little they had, so they weren't afraid Traveler might be competition.

Traveler skidded forty feet down the hillside. He hesitated, controlling his temper, making certain his expression was impassive. Then he walked toward them.

They were thirty feet away now.

"Couple of salvagers here, tried to get the drop on us," Harry explained as Traveler walked toward them.

Traveler kept coming. Silently.

"The girl here had a knife," Joe offered.

Traveler kept coming, walking slowly and evenly.

"The old fellow, he had a bow and arrow. We figure they were fixing to ambush us," Harry said.

Traveler walked up to them, saying nothing at all.

"Now what I figure is—" Harry began.

Traveler snapped the butt of the rifle up and cold-cocked Harry, neat and clean. Harry toppled like a side of beef dropped from a truck.

"Hey—" Joe began, raising the M16. "What'd you do that f—"

That's when Traveler knocked the barrel of the M16 aside and kicked out, sinking the steel toe of his boot in Joe's groin. Joe doubled over, making a strangely high-pitched yipping sound. When he bent double he met Traveler's knee on its way up. The knee caught Joe on the point of his chin and sent him over backward onto his butt.

Traveler's finger trembled on the trigger of the rifle. But he forced himself to put it aside, laying it down beside the fallen M16.

He waited.

Joe got loggily to his feet. He shook himself like a dazed bull. He was a big guy, and he was mad. He charged Traveler, snorting like a bull as he came. Traveler let himself be seen as a target, let Joe think he was going to be there to stomp—and at the last split second he ducked to a low squat, grabbed Joe's ankles, lifted, and pushed off. Joe's momentum carried him over Traveler's

49

head, and Traveler tilted him so the big man fell hard, almost vertically

Traveler let go and danced back, as Joe, stunned, blinking but enraged, got up and charged him again. He came more slowly this time, and Traveler sidestepped him easily, then kicked him hard in the ass to send him sprawling again—atop Harry, who was just beginning to sit up.

The two men thrashed together in hurt confusion for a moment, then Joe rolled off Harry and sat on his ass, knees drawn up, head in his arms, looking like he was going to cry.

Traveler drew his boot knife, stepped in close, took Joe by the hair, and yanked his head back. He pressed the point of the knife to Joe's throat.

"Understand me," Traveler said. "You are either going to do what I tell you, or I'm going to stomp you again, and then I'm going to kill you. Kill you dead. You doubt I can do it?" He pressed the point an eighth of an inch into the skin of Joe's neck. A small trickle of blood oozed down.

Joe croaked out, "Okay. Sure."

"Good," Traveler went on. "Now listen . . ." He paused to back up and pick up the rifle without turning his back to the two men. "From now on you don't fire those guns unless I tell you to. Understand? You don't mess with anybody unless I send you to mess with them. Okay?"

They nodded dumbly.

He held the rifle in one hand; with the other he sheathed the knife. "Now I know what you're thinking. 'Just wait till this asshole turns his back.' Right? Forget it. I know when a man is doing something behind my back. I have that power." He said it with total conviction, and it was part of the legend about him. They believed it. "And more important, you need me. If you go back to your settlement without those horses and without the car, who are they gonna blame, huh?"

Joe and Harry looked at one another.

"That's right," Traveler said. "They'll blame you. Stick with me and I'll get you what you want."

But he'd already decided that once these slobs were no longer useful, he was going to do the world a favor.

The three men trudged along the thin trail that paralleled the road. It was a hot morning. The sun was baking the backs of their necks. The rifles were hot and heavy in their hands. All three men were battered, and there was no love lost between them.

Traveler, in particular, was feeling rocky. His head wound had festered, and he felt weak and sick. It was hard in this heat to tell if he had a fever, but he suspected he did. And it was a long way to the next pharmacist. Maybe five thousand miles away, down to the southern hemisphere. Brazil was supposed to be relatively intact. . . .

He wondered idly if the southern hemisphere would provide the new cradle of civilization. Major civilizations had arisen before in South America. But, of course, after the Third World War the world's economy had fallen apart. Massive ecological disruptions had followed, and the relatively radiation-free southern hemisphere had suffered massively from the sudden cutoff of aid from the more developed countries, the droughts and other weather madnesses, the ash-blackened skies, the famines and endless, debilitating strings of revolutions. Maybe by now, though, they'd have begun to get it together. Maybe a New Inca Empire would arise. . . .

He thought about these things to keep from dwelling on the pain. His head felt like it had a colony of termites in it chewing their way out.

But he showed none of the signs of weariness outwardly. He knew it was important he keep up a strong front around Joe and Harry. He began to wonder if he hadn't made a

51

major mistake in letting them come along. Maybe they'd be more trouble than help. Still, they'd fought well enough against the roadrats.

His thoughts went around and around like that, his feet trudged, the sweat dripped, the pain throbbed, the day got older.

Traveler hoped they might catch up with the Meat Wagon in Drift. But no, the hijacker wouldn't stay there long. He'd be going on to rejoin his people.

It looked bad. He'd need the antitoxin soon.

"What's that?" Joe said suddenly, pointing off to the right.

"What do you mean, 'What's that?' " Harry said irritably. "That's what people call 'smoke.' "

Traveler looked. A thin strand of blue smoke was rising like a swami's rope trick above a stand of stubby, blue-needled Joshua trees a hundred yards to the west. Traveler felt a tingle of premonition. . . .

For a moment all was still as the three men gazed at the thread of smoke. It could be anything, that smoke. The beginning of a brushfire. Or a roadrat encampment. A survivors' colony on some salvaging expedition. Bloats. Glory Boys. Bikers.

And it just might be the guerrillas.

There could be a connecting road from the highway to a camp in those woods. . . .

No, probably the hijacker had gone on to Drift.

Traveler turned away—and froze. Distantly, faintly, they heard the neighing of horses.

Traveler turned and started cross-country to the woods. Harry and Joe looked at one another, then started after him.

When they got to the outlying trees, Traveler turned to them and clipped out, "You hang back about three minutes, then cut north and come in from the opposite side. Unless

52

somebody fires on you, don't start shooting till you hear my signal." He slapped the assault rifle. "This will give you the signal. Come in shooting when you hear my first burst. You got it?"

Joe swallowed. He nodded. Harry nodded, too, but there was something about his expression Traveler didn't like. It was no expression at all. That emptiness was a cover-up. "Forget it, Harry, whatever you're thinking," Traveler said sharply.

Harry reddened.

"Don't forget, wait three minutes." Traveler turned and loped into the woods. He had a strange feeling that Harry and Joe weren't going to make it through the day alive. They were blunderers. Probably the guerrillas would get 'em. Which meant it was a good thing he'd left the gas can buried with the other supplies back near the wrecked car. He could reclaim them for himself later.

In the coolness of the woods Traveler was quite sure he had a fever. He could feel it in his throat like a flame licking up inside a stovepipe. He was dizzy and nauseated, and his head throbbed. But he had to find the Meat Wagon. And the antitoxin.

The pines and Joshua trees were dense enough to screen him but dispersed enough to allow him easy passage. Fallen needles crackled underfoot. A flutter of motion seen out of the corner of one eye made him turn, gun ready to blast. But it was just a bird—a mutated bird with a strangely human face, staring at him from a tree branch. He and the bird stared at one another. It had fleshy skin instead of feathers on its head; small, thin lips instead of a beak; and otherwise looked like an owl. Its tiny lips moved, and he thought he heard it say, "Shumi, the old priest with the mountainous cat, he sent me to warn you. To tell you this: that The Black Rider is stalking you and looks for his chance to destroy you."

Traveler's legendary cool vanished. He gaped openly.

The bird became a blur of wings, flying away. It was gone.

Hallucinating, Traveler thought. A fever dream.

He hurried on, remembering that he'd given Joe and Harry just three minutes to get to the camp fire, if that's what it was.

A minute later he was crouching behind a thatch of large purple sagebrush, looking out on a sunny clearing. The air was dusty and redolent of tree pitch and burning pine. Two horses were tied up on the far side of the clearing. Smoke rose from a camp fire. It was a small fire and nothing was cooking on it—what use was it on this hot day? Then he saw a figure clad in brown-and-green camouflage-patterned fatigues come out of an old gray canvas tent, carrying a piece of cardboard. Whoever it was had his back to him. A slender sort of guy. Traveler couldn't see him clearly—a strange blue fog was filling his eyes. Steam from the fever, he thought. He strained his eyes to make out a dark rectangular shape at the other end of the clearing. Yeah, that was it.

The Meat Wagon.

Two more people came out of the tent, an old woman and a boy of about fourteen.

The hijacker was doing something at the fire with the flap of cardboard. Waving it over the smoke. Strange thing to do.

Traveler looked around and saw no one else. No reason this couldn't be a bloodless recapture of the van.

He moved forward in a crouch, came within five feet of the three figures by the fire, stopped, stood up, raised his rifle, and said, "Okay, be very cool. Turn around real slowly."

The old woman and the kid turned and looked at him.

The hijacker tossed the cardboard aside, stood, and slowly turned around.

A woman. An Indian woman. A beautiful elfin face. Copper skin. Golden brown eyes; high cheekbones; full, delicate lips; short, man-cut black hair. No more than twenty years old. Slender and—he could see it now, at this range—shapely.

Traveler looked into her eyes, expecting to see murderous rage, madness, or fanaticism. He saw only the determined burning of a will to survive.

"I, uh . . ." he began, licking his lips. She had stolen his van—so why did he feel this impulse to apologize?

And then the gunfire erupted from the woods.

Harry and Joe came running out, hooting, M16s blazing.

"Get out of the way, Traveler!" Harry shouted. "We'll get 'em!"

The slugs punched the arid ground between Traveler and the three strangers, kicking up little spires of dust. The old woman and the boy screamed and threw themselves down. The old woman tried to cover the boy, and the boy tried to cover the old woman. The hijacker looked uncertainly from Traveler to Harry and Joe.

"Get out of the way, Traveler!" Joe shouted.

But Traveler stepped between the hijacker and the two oncoming men.

They skidded to a stop, guns ready at their hips, gaping in confusion.

"What do you—"

"Think you're—"

"Doing?"

—the two men asked.

Traveler answered them: "I had a feeling you two assholes weren't going to make it through the day."

He snapped the assault rifle up and cut loose, spraying back and forth, zigzagging the full auto-bursts so that they slashed the two men to bloody pieces. Harry tried to return fire as the slugs staggered him backward; his shots racketed harmlessly into the treetops, and he fell. The gun clattered to the ground. Joe went spinning into death, falling in an ungainly heap.

Shaking with fury, dizzy, light-headed, Traveler emptied the clip into the two bodies, just lifeless bags of wet meat now.

Traveler dropped the gun and turned, swaying, to the hijacker. She was gazing at him with open curiosity.

"I—" he began. He coughed. The words were trapped in his throat. He forced them out. "I'm sorry but . . . I've got to take my van back. . . ."

The blue fog closed in, and he felt weightless. It was a minute before he'd realized he'd fallen over. He tried to get up and couldn't. The blue fog became black.

# 7

## The Hijacker

A thought was drifting through his mind. It was like a cloud with a small gaseous body all its own, smoky gray against the blue-black background of his semiconsciousness: Smoke signals. With the fire and the cardboard flap. She was making smoke signals.

Then, as if that thought were the combination that opened the lock and let him out into consciousness, he opened his eyes and blinked away shreds of blue fog. He was lying on his back. Overhead were five intersecting lines. A blue-metal line intersecting with the lines of canvas folds. The interior of the tent top.

"They didn't kill me," he murmured wonderingly. In the background, someone laughed.

He felt unreal and dry, brittle as an old stick bleached two years in the desert sun. It was hot in the tent.

"Since you're not gonna kill me," he said raspily, "can you give me a little water?"

"Don't be so sure we won't kill you," said a husky woman's voice, from somewhere out of his line of sight. "Maybe we're saving you to stake to an anthill." More laughter. The boy, laughing.

But he heard a reassuring clinking sound and then someone bent over him, holding out a tin cup. It was just a tin cup with a little water beaded on its side, but at that moment it was more beautiful than the crown jewels. He got up on one elbow and reached out, taking the cup, drinking deeply.

"Not too much yet," she said, taking the cup away before he'd have preferred. "Lay back down," she said. The hijacker.

The hijacker, he thought, is beautiful.

He glanced at the other two. A leathery-faced crone with stringy white hair but bright, intelligent black eyes, and a slender Indian boy in a loincloth. There was paint daubed on his cheeks, red and yellow stripes, and a feather hung down aslant behind his right ear. He had a slightly crooked smile and impudent gray eyes. Only the old woman looked like purebred Indian.

"What tribe?" he asked.

"Cheyenne," the hijacker said. "Now lay down or you get the anthill."

He lay back on the sleeping bag. "My name's . . ." He almost said, Kiel Paxton. He had a powerful urge to tell them his real name. But he conjured up his usual reserve and said, "Traveler."

The young woman's eyes widened, just slightly. "Oh— yes? I'm Jan. This is Striking Snake. We call him Snake. And Face Cloud. It's she who is healing you."

"Healing me? What's wrong with me?"

The boy laughed. "He's a funny one, this man."

"Blood poisoning," the old woman said. "Infection. We drew it out with herbs. Wait."

She went from the tent and returned a moment later with something hot in a clay cup. "Drink it," she said, "and don't fuck around. Drink it all down fast."

He got up on his elbow again and took the cup.

The smell from the cup was heart-stopping. But he drank, forcing the vile effluvium down. "Ugh," he said.

"*We'll* make with the old-fashioned Indian talk," Face Cloud said. "*You* shut up and lay back."

He lay back, his head whirling. "What's in that stuff?"

"Garlic, goldenseal, bee propolis, and some stuff you don't want to know about."

"They take bee propolis from beehives," the boy said, "and the bees use it to keep enemies out of the hive. In the belly it keeps the unwanted enemies out too."

"Evil spirits?" Traveler asked, trying to play along.

"Bacterium!" the boy said, as if amazed at Traveler's ignorance. "Microbes of all kinds. Didn't anyone ever teach you anything?"

"Not . . . much. . . ." Traveler said. He felt weak. The world was slipping away again.

"Sleep now," Face Cloud said.

He did as he was told.

The blue fog closed in again, condensing till it became black.


When he woke again it was night. The only light was a muted yellow glow from a kerosene lamp at his feet.

A man was frowning down at him. An Indian. He looked as if he didn't approve of Traveler at all. He was young, maybe younger than Jan, with a squat face and long black braids. He wore a leather jacket, fatigues, and combat boots. He was squatting on his haunches.

Traveler was thirsty again, but he couldn't bring himself to ask this dour Indian for a glass of water. So he said, "Hello. I'm Traveler."

"Yes," the man said. There was a long silence.

Traveler tried again. "They said you're Cheyenne. A bit far north and west for Cheynne, aren't you?"

"The old tribal grounds were desecrated. Anyway, no one tells the Indians where to go now. We go where we damn please."

Traveler could identify with that.

"I guess you people plan to sell me to the army, since you're keeping me alive," Traveler said.

The Indian looked thoughtful. "That hadn't occurred to me. Not a bad idea. Yes, we might . . ."

Traveler groaned inwardly.

But the Indian sighed and went on: "Knife Wind won't allow it, though. Jan's his daughter and he dotes on her, and she's got other plans for you."

"Like what?"

The Indian looked at him sharply. "She'll tell you when she feels like it. Now—hold out your hands, wrists together." He had a length of rawhide in his hand.

Traveler hesitated. Maybe he should gather his strength and make his move now. Knock this guy down and run for it. He flexed his muscles as he slowly lifted his hands up, wrists together. No, he was still too weak. This Indian would be no pushover. He allowed his wrists to be tied. But they weren't tied for long.

"Cut him loose," said a voice from the tent door-flap. A voice like a crow. The two men looked. It was Face Cloud, scowling.

The brave returned the scowl. "He's too dangerous to go untied."

"When he was asleep he spoke," the old woman said. "He spoke his dreams. The owl-with-a-man's-face has come to him and warned him. If the owl comes to him, he has strong medicine. This man has damn *strong* medicine! He is to be an honored guest."

"Look, Face, the omens from dream stuff just doesn't cut it anymore—"

"Listen, Danny: Do as I tell you. This man saved our lives."

Snorting with disgust, Danny cut the bonds and left the tent.

60

The old woman came and looked at Traveler closely. She felt his pulse. Then she asked, "You hungry?"

"Yes. Thanks. And thirsty as all hell."

She went out, and there was talk by the fire. He couldn't make out what was being said. There were the voices of several men, arguing. So the raiders had returned. Maybe the whole tribe was here. Good thing he hadn't made that move on Danny. Even if he'd succeeded, the others would have cut him down.

Jan—the "hijacker"—came in carrying a clay bowl of rabbit stew and a tin cup of water. She set it beside him, gave him a mess-kit spoon, and watched him as he sat up and ate.

Afterward he felt immeasurably better. Better than he'd felt in a long time. The headache was gone. But now that the mists of sleep were evaporated, he could feel the neurotoxin damage coming back at him like the distant whine of a train approaching a long way down a dark tunnel.

"How you feel?" Jan asked.

"Better. Thanks. But there's one thing I need bad—a medicine. In the van's fridge unit. The little vials."

"Okay—what is it?"

"An antitoxin. I had heavy nerve damage a long time ago from an army neurotoxin. Without the antitoxin I . . . lose control."

"But where'd you get medicine like that?"

"Just before the war I was in a VA hospital. The antitoxin was experimental. They tried it on me and it worked. They had a big batch of it made up, to be shipped out to other hospitals. But then the war hit. I knew what was coming down, so I grabbed the antitoxin supply and the formula and the unit it was in. I stole a car and fought my way cross-country, between the blasts, wearing a radiation suit. Stole that too. I found the lab out in New Mexico where they made the stuff. The lab is still there, still standing.

There was more of the stuff there and every so often I go back and stock up on it.''

''Where'd you get the van?''

''Out of a car showroom in a deserted town. Just stumbled on it by luck. Rebuilt it.''

''I see that. I'll get the stuff.''

She went out, returned five minutes later with the antitoxin.

He swallowed a hit, corked it, and handed it back to her.

''Did you ever wonder,'' she said, ''if you really need the stuff?''

He was startled. ''What?''

''I mean, maybe you're kind of psychologically hung up on it. It's been years now, right? Probably by now the neurotoxins have been washed out by the antitoxin and all the intervening time. Maybe the antitoxin has a slight narcoticizing effect.''

He stared at her. ''Where'd you learn those words? You were only maybe five when the war came down. There hasn't been a school open since, except maybe in Kansas City or Wichita. They wouldn't have let you in.''

''I figure you're asking me that to change the subject. But—it was the Chief who taught me. He had a degree in psychology. He specialized in rehabilitating alcoholic Indians before the war. He teaches school here. Or wherever we are. We've got a lot of books stashed away too.'' Seeing his expression, she smiled. ''You thought the Indians would just 'go back to the land'? We're not stupid enough to throw away the good things the white man brought us, just because he brought us a lot of bad things too.''

Traveler felt strange. Something—funny, odd-feeling—in his face. Then he realized what it was. He was smiling. A large, free sort of smile. It had been years since he'd smiled that way, and the muscles of his face weren't used to it. They were used to a sort of grim flicker of amusement, at best.

"You know," Jan said, "you're not bad-looking when you smile. A little grizzled. What a shame white men grow all that ugly hair on their faces. Well, the Chief's got a straight razor. Normally he keeps it for cutting throats. Maybe he'll let you borrow it for shaving. If he decides not to cut your throat with it."

Traveler stopped smiling.

"If you need to piss," Jan said matter-of-factly, "there's a hollowed gourd over there. You can't go outside till tomorrow. And there'll be guards at the tent all night. The Chief doesn't usually trust white men, but I talked to him and he just might let you off."

"And if he decides I'm a problem?"

"He'll probably sell you to the army. G'night."

# 8

## Two Men, Two Missions

Major Vallone was unhappy with the state of things. Just now, he was pissed off because the automatic food dispenser wasn't working. Again. And what really bugged him was that the machine wasn't alive; therefore, he couldn't kill it. He couldn't even smash it, because General Harker'd have his ass for it. All he could do was fume impotently and give the thing a toe-stinging kick.

He was in the dispensary of Base Zero, three hundred feet beneath the sands of the Mojave desert, fifty miles north of where Las Vegas used to be. Things were constantly breaking down in the dispensary, and everywhere else in the base. The food was lousy. The ersatz coffee tasted like oil. The plants in the hydroponic gardens had died because of tainted water, and there were no fresh vegetables. They were all eating ancient K-rations and freeze-dried crap again. And on top of it all, Harker was threatening to close down Vallone's baby, Special Project 77. SP77 was Vallone's stepping-stone to power. And wasn't that what was really bugging Harker?

Sure it was.

Either that or he was going soft. All this talk about "the danger of further decimation of the civilian population" was sickening.

Vallone was a stubby, gray-haired man with a pencil-line mustache. And cold eyes. He turned those eyes on the young man who strode up to him now. Wentworth. Weedy little guy, Vallone thought. Might be useful, though. The little slime's got ambition.

"Excuse me, Major Vallone—"

"Yeah—what do you want?" Vallone snapped, turning his icy eyes on Wentworth.

Wentworth, a lieutenant, shivered.

"It's General Harker, sir. He'd like to see you."

"Oh, yeah? I'm honored. Lead me there." He knew perfectly well where Harker's office was, but he wanted a chance to talk to Wentworth.

The two men strolled side by side down the steel hallway. The fluorescent lights overhead, powered by the nuclear reactor in the sub-basement, flickered and buzzed. The buzz and their footsteps were the only sounds here.

Until Vallone's soft aside, "Lieutenant—"

*"What?"* Wentworth, startled, jumped a little. "I mean, uh—sir?"

Vallone smiled. "How would you like to advance in rank and get some special privileges? I've seen the way you've been looking at the Recreation Girls. I can arrange it."

"Oh, uh—thank you, sir." Wentworth waited. He wasn't stupid.

"Wentworth, just between you and me, do you think Harker's doing a good job?"

Wentworth hesitated and scratched his thin, pimply cheek.

Harker was not popular with the men. No one in charge would be popular with the men. Just as any president who has the bad luck to be elected when forces beyond his control ordain a depression will be blamed for that depression, so Harker was blamed for the all-around shabbiness of the living quarters, the bad quality of the food, and the special privileges that the president's closest men kept mostly for themselves. So Vallone knew that it would be easy to find someone who was willing to knock Harker. If he could get the guy to be honest about his feelings. "Well, sir, it's not for me to say—"

"Come on, Wentworth. I'm not testing you. *I* think Harker's an inefficient stumblebum." Vallone put his hand on the younger man's thin shoulder. "You can tell me."

Wentworth looked around, then said in a low voice. "I'd have to agree with you, sir. He's a real jerk."

"Right. But you know how it is with this power elite. Hard to get them out of the way, right? Extreme measures are necessary. Got to do a little conniving below board at times for the greater good, right? Now, if you want that promotion and those special privileges, all you have to do is"—he took a small cellophane package from his pocket—"put this in the general's desk drawer. You're his assistant, you'll have a chance. Then we give Security a tip that there's drugs being used illegally in that office and . . . well, they'll find them. You know how the president is about drugs. He's real uptight about them. Security reports on drug abuse directly to him. And then Harker'll be out of the way and you and I can move up. . . ."

Trembling, Wentworth accepted the package.

And he nodded once. That was enough.

They turned a corner in the hall and came to Harker's office.

Inside, they found Harker scowling over a sheaf of papers laid out on the big gray steel desk. Harker was a tall, rawboned man with bushy white eyebrows and trembling hands. Would the president believe such a man was a drug user? Poke Frayling in his paranoia and he would believe anything about anyone, given even the mildest evidence.

Harker got right to it.

"Vallone, I've been reading your recommendation for expansion of SP77. Far from recommending that myself, I'm going to suggest that we close it down."

Vallone said, controlling his tone, "And why is that, sir?"

"This Neurotoxin 77. Now, if I understand your plan right, you're going to drop it on one of the settlements near Kansas City, to give the people thereabouts a taste of what the stuff is like, and then demand that Kansas City and the other colonies and settlements recognize the authority of the president or get a nice big dose of NT77 themselves. Correct?"

"Essentially."

"First of all, the stuff hasn't been tested under controlled conditions—"

"It was tested in El Hiagura. It proved out. It drives men insane. If they don't claw themselves to death, they go into catatonia or become worthless freakos. It would be the end of any place we dumped it on. And it would be an end in a nasty way—that would make a point. We need to terrorize them into it—"

"Vallone, the testing in El Hiagura was performed by a hostile government. We don't know for sure what the stuff did there. They didn't clue us in. The people we've tested it on here have responded variously. Some seem to have a resistance to it. It wears off on some. Some react as you described. Even if it works, it's no way to make a working relationship with the civilian population. I recommend we forget it."

"Do you? We'll see what the president says. Sir."

Vallone turned on his heel and went out. Harker watched him, sighing.

Wentworth cleared his throat. "Uh—do you need me for something, sir?"

Harker shot him a dark look. "Yeah. Clean up my

67

office. I'm going to the Rec Center.'' He got up, put on his coat—the center's air-conditioning worked *too* well—and went out.

Wentworth opened the general's desk drawer and put something in it.

Then he went to the phone and dialed a number. ''Hello—Security?''

Jan on one side of him, Danny on the other, Traveler walked across the clearing to the Chief's tent. It was a waterproofed canvas tent like the others but larger and tepee-shaped, painted with Indian pictoglyphs.

There were twenty tents pitched around the clearing now, and more horses were tied up under the trees. Sentries stood guard at the camp's perimeters. One sat on a platform of woven branches high in a pine, watching for roadrats, Bloats, army, or vagabonds. The sunlight was bright, making Traveler shade his eyes. He felt a little weak but ready for action.

Chief Knife Wind was sitting under a horsehide awning, which was stretched over sharpened sticks stuck in the ground just outside the entrance to his tent. He was cleaning a gun. The gun was Traveler's .45.

Traveler didn't like the proprietary way the Chief was cleaning it.

The Chief was a short, stocky man with sun-darkened red skin creased with so many lines it was difficult to make out his expressions. He seemed distantly amused by everything. He wore the same green-and-brown combat suit the others wore, and a triple-feather headdress; long white braids dangled over the gun-cleaning rods in his hand. He laid the gun and cleaning rods aside and looked Traveler up and down. Finally he said, ''You look like you might actually be capable of some of the things attributed to you." His voice might have been a lawyer's; it was incongruous with his appearance.

Traveler regarded him evenly. He waited.

Knife Wind said, "Have a seat." He gestured to a pallet beside him. There was room for two in the shade of the awning. Traveler sat.

"I value the counsel of my daughter and of Face Cloud immensely," Knife Wind said, taking a joint from a shirt pocket. He lit up, sucked smoke, and passed it to Traveler. Traveler puffed on it but didn't actually inhale. He passed it back. "These two wise demigoddesses," Knife Wind went on, "advise me to allow you to live. And to be given a choice: Go free or work with us. . . . Tell me this: Is it true you are a friend of the priest Shumi, he of the mountainous cat?"

Traveler said, "We've met. I owe him a favor, in fact. I guess we're allies."

Knife Wind watched him closely as he spoke. "I always know when a man is lying. You are not. Any friend of Shumi's is a friend of mine. Shumi is a great holy man. His medicine knocks my socks off. Therefore, you may live and go free."

"With my van," Traveler said. "And my weapons."

The Chief looked at him with what might have been genuine surprise. "Are you serious, sir? The rules of the world as it is now dictate that what a man takes he may keep. And, of course, you stole those things yourself."

"I found the van deserted. Salvaged it."

"The distinction is superfluous. The van is ours . . . unless, of course, you'd care to . . . earn it back."

Traveler waited.

Knife Wind took another hit, exhaled blue smoke, and went on, "My son, Martin Luther King Plainwalker, was kidnapped by men who sold him to the army. I want him back. His sister Jan has a scheme for getting him back. We have learned that the army, in its salvage operation, has recently come across a neurotoxin-storage warehouse in one of their deserted bases. They have taken possession of this stuff and moved it to a place near their Base Zero. They apparently have big plans for it—and they are searching for a second warehouse which was referred to in records they found at the first. They know it exists but not exactly where. My people stumbled on this second nerve-gas warehouse. The nerve gas, Neurotoxin 77, can be rendered harmless when subjected to great heat. We burned the place down and destroyed the gas as a matter of principle.'' He sighed. ''It required considerable soul-searching first—I might have made a great profit on the stuff. At any rate, we destroyed the toxin, except for one small, labeled canister. We intend to use this to bargain our way into close proximity with the army camp where slaves are kept. And there we hope to liberate my son.''

''Why not simply trade the canister for him?''

''It isn't enough. They want the location of the warehouse. They don't know we destroyed it. They insist on checking it out before letting him go. So, we will say that our emissaries will deal only with their top man, who works everyday in the slave camp, overseeing them. A Major Vallone.''

Traveler stiffened. ''Vallone . . .''

''Yes. Our 'emissaries' go in to make the deal—and then liberate the prison camp from the inside, commando-style. My daughter Jan is the one they know. They will only tolerate one other to go in with her. I have picked you because you know military setups, I suspect. You were a military man, were you not?''

Traveler nodded. ''I also know NT77.''

''To be honest, another reason I picked you is, I don't want to risk any more of my own people. Danny will lead a squadron that will be available for backup, however, outside the gates. And if you can arm the prisoners—"

Traveler said, "The odds are still long against us."

"Yes. I can offer you, in addition to the van and your weapons, a tank of gas and all the food you can carry. And what ammo we have that matches your ordnance."

Traveler smiled. "I'll take it. But now that the deal is sealed, I can tell you, you didn't have to offer that much. I was going there, anyway. To get Vallone. This gives me the perfect chance."

Knife Wind nodded. "Some chessmaster has brought you here. Some destiny overlord. Some spirit."

Traveler shrugged. Then he said, "I'll need the Meat Wagon for the trip. There's a lot of dangerous ground to cover before Base Zero."

"The Meat Wagon? Oh! That is what you call the van? Charming. But how will I know that you won't steal it away?"

Traveler let out a long breath. "I agree to go through with the mission, all the way, even if you give me the van out front. If you know when a man is lying, then look in my eyes, tell me if I'm lying now."

Knife Wind looked. "Okay," he said. "You got it. Want another hit of this?"


The open road. It felt good.

Traveler could feel it humming beneath the tires of the Meat Wagon. He sat behind the wheel. Jan sat beside him. Behind, hidden in a cabinet, was a two-foot by eight-inch canister of NT77, the stuff that had made Traveler's life hell fifteen years before.

"How often do you take the antitoxin?" Jan asked, out of the blue.

"What? Oh, every few days maybe, every few weeks, usually. I once went a month without it."

71

"Not definitely? It varies?"

"Yeah. Why?"

"Does the need for it come at any particular time? I mean for example, like when you're under great stress?"

"Uh. I don't know. Maybe."

"You don't like this subject much, do you."

"No," he admitted.

"That tells me something too."

Her analytical self-assurance annoyed him. But it was difficult to stay annoyed with her long. One look at her and the irritation melted away. She didn't talk much, and he liked that. This was their first conversation in an hour. They were comfortable together. And she was a better fighter than ninety-five percent of the men on the road. She was something else. She was . . .

Traveler thought, Uh-oh.

It was a sun-spattered morning with small clouds breaking up the light and chasing each other across a candy-blue sky. The desert unrolled around them with a certain naked magnificence. Drift was a mile or two up ahead. They had business there. . . .

Traveler glanced at her and wondered what would happen between them.


The Black Rider was black, truly black, blacker in every way than the man who stood before him. The man was an "Afro American," a tall, gaunt, tired-eyed man with pock-marked cheeks. He didn't seem afraid of the Black Rider, which was strange.

Everyone was afraid of the Black Rider.

The Black Rider was lean and bald. Hairless. No fat on him. Lithe cat-muscle. His eyes were black—there were no whites at all. Just orbs of onyx. There was no white or pink on him, not at lips or hands. He was simply black, and dressed neck to toe in black leather.

He straddled his black motorcycle, a 1988 S. C. Wilson Harley, propped in the mouth of an old mineshaft he made his home. The chocolate-colored man said, "I heard you were looking for me."

"I don't have to look for you. I know where you are, where everyone is I have need of." A voice like steel wool on glass.

The brown man waited for the black man to say more.

At last the black mutant—he was far from human—leaned back against the bar on the end of the big bike's seat and said dreamily, "There is a man I want dead. More than dead, I want him crushed. More than crushed, I want him shamed. He thwarted me and destroyed my followers."

"Who is this man?"

"He calls himself Traveler."

The brown man frowned. "I've heard about him. From what I've heard, he's a decent guy. There aren't enough left." He shook his head. "I can't do it, man."

The Black Rider eased forward and leaned his elbows casually on the handlebars.

The brown man tried to look away. He couldn't.

He made a small, soft sound, all that escaped his lips of the shout of anger boiling inside him.

And then the Black Rider reached out; he reached out without moving so much as an inch. He arms remained where they were. He reached out with his mind and snared the unprepared mind of the brown man, attached puppet strings to it, and took firm hold on those strings.

"He's coming now, down the highway north of Drift. Stop him and kill him."

The brown man turned and walked stiffly out of the mineshaft entrance and on down the hill.

*     *     *

73

"Drift is just around that bend," Jan was saying. "We can meet the army rep there, in the trading depot—"

She broke off, seeing the thing that was blocking the road up ahead.

It was a semitruck tractor, without the trailer. It was big, it was mean-looking. Traveler just didn't like the looks of it.

It was sitting squarely in their way, as if waiting for them. The windows were polarized: he couldn't see the driver. It was as if the big semi was a living thing with a will of its own, self-driven. Its blackened vertical exhaust pipe snorted out blue-black smoke as they came around the bend.

And then it charged.

# 9

## A Suburb of Drift Called Death

It was a bulldog of a GMC, big slabs of metal plating bolted on it for crude armor. Metal mesh—as on the Meat Wagon—hung down to protect the wheels. Enormous wheels. Each tire five feet high. The metal plates were rusted, and what could be seen of the original cab was red. Light lanced off the windshield as the big truck came on. Smoke trailed thickly from its chimney.

It was about fifty yards away and closing, picking up speed. There was no mistaking that approach—the driver had every intention of stomping the Meat Wagon under his wheels.

The highway cut through a hill here; sheer rock walls enclosed the road. There was no question of going off into the desert. There was no time to back up. But the semitruck tractor outweighed the Meat Wagon by at least a ton. Its front fenders had been replaced by a sharp, steel-ramming wedge. To either side of the wedge were a couple of four-inch-thick steel spikes, angling to slash anything that passed within eight inches.

And now, poking from a metal slot cut under the windshield, in the center of the cab, was the snout of a submachine gun.

Traveler didn't wonder *why* the trucker had decided to

go for him. He met more adversaries on the road than allies. This was probably another road pirate hoping to loot the van for whatever it held of value. And indifferent to the thing in the van Traveler regarded as most valuable: his life.

Traveler glanced at Jan. She was already feeding a clip into the light assault rifle. There wasn't a trace of panic on her face. All she said was, "I wonder where he gets the diesel. . . ."

The highway was two lanes wide, but the semi was coming down it hell-bent-for-leather in the dead center, taking up a big chunk of both lanes.

Traveler's only advantage was speed.

He shifted gears to high and floored it. He headed down the center line as if planning to kamikaze the semi head-on.

Jan glanced at him, raised an eyebrow, and shrugged. She climbed in the back to put the snout of the Armalite through a firing slit between two of the bullet-proof vests Traveler used as partial armor. She crouched directly behind Traveler, waiting.

The semi loomed up ahead, gnashing metallically as it changed for a higher gear, coming at them about 65 mph now. If it hit them it would smash the Meat Wagon like an empty beer can under a boot heel.

Traveler drove straight for it. Playing chicken. But knowing that the semi wouldn't veer off first. He could feel it. The guy was coming at him single-mindedly. To kill.

Traveler's knuckles were white on the wheel. He leaned forward in his seat, his teeth clamped, eyes locked on the enemy's windshield. The Meat Wagon was roaring along at ninety, ninety-five . . .

The semi was almost on top of them.

He could feel Jan tense behind him. But she didn't say a word.

Five seconds to impact. Four, three, two, and—

Traveler cut right, swerving, scratching black rubber on the road as he swerved around the semi, so close that the spikes, protruding like tusks from the bumpers, scraped two long gouges in the side of the Meat Wagon. The Armalite rattled. And then they'd shot past the semi; they were humming down the road, in the clear.

He let out a breath and looked in his rearview mirror. The semi was barreling along, not having room to turn around quickly. It passed out of the restricting walls where the road cut through the hill and slowed to turn. But he'd be long gone by the time it got turned around and tried to pursue.

"How'd you figure that out?" Jan asked, looking out a firing slit in the back doors.

"I figured if I came on like I was going to try to pass him, he'd wait till I was almost there and then veer over. I had to make him think I was going to play either chicken or kamikaze. So I could keep him in the center of the road where I knew I could pass him. Otherwise he'd have swung over and blocked my lane. And I counted on the Wagon's speed to get around him before he had time to recover."

"He's turning around, back there."

Up ahead of the Meat Wagon, the highway vanished.

It vanished in an explosion, a double explosion that took out the concrete overpass over the dry wash. The overpass crumpled into the wash, leaving ragged edges and a thirty-foot gap. Smoke and dust billowed up, undulating.

Traveler hit the brakes, and the van squealed, then spun, skating all the way around twice before coming to a stop a foot from the edge of the gap in the road.

It was fifty feet down to a tumble of sharp-edged boulders, beyond that verge.

Traveler, recovering from the wrenching inertia of the sudden stop, glimpsed a dark figure on the highway, beyond the hole in the overpass. A figure so black he might have been a silhouette cut from a sheet of ebony, riding away on a big black motorcycle, seen dimly through the veil of smoke.

Traveler seemed to hear ghostly laughter echo in his ears. And then the dark rider was gone.

But the semitruck tractor was rumbling up from behind.

This time Jan was startled. "Who blew up the road?"

"An old 'friend' of mine. Looks like he's setting me up to even a score."

Traveler backed up, turned the van to face the semi. The enigmatic juggernaut rolled implacably toward them. "We meet again," Traveler murmured.

"What about the overhead guns?" Jan asked.

"At the angle they're set up, they wouldn't hit that windshield. Which might be bullet-proof, anyway. And he's heavily armored. . . . You do any damage with that rifle?"

"Don't think so. I shot for the wheels but I think I hit the rims."

"Here he comes. Hold on!"

There was about ten feet between the edge of the dry-wash canyon and the rock of the hillside. Traveler swung the van left, driving overland, parallel to the canyon's drop-off. The ground was rocky. The Meat Wagon jumped and rollicked. They risked a broken axle and blown tires. But the semi was roaring down on them from behind. Traveler looked in the side-mounted rearview. The semi was turning off the road, spitting up dust as it ground its huge wheels into the desert. It was only about thirty feet behind. He could almost feel hot breath on the back of his neck.

The Meat Wagon's speed advantage didn't mean much here. The rough terrain slowed him up too much. The semi seemed to barrel over it with no trouble. As he watched, the big truck crunched over a twenty-foot tree, leaving it splintered behind, roaring on. Traveler had to veer left to avoid a big saguaro. The truck ran right over it.

An ear-splitting series of *thwangs* reverberated as the semi opened up on the rear of the Meat Wagon with its machine gun. The rear window shattered, and the bullet-proof vests layered against the back door leaped, punching inward as the big slugs hammered through to them. They held, but if the truck got much nearer the close range would probably give the slugs the power to smash through the van's makeshift armor.

Risking the axle damage, Traveler stepped on the gas, pulling ahead, cutting around boulders, trying to keep as many obstacles as possible between him and the juggernaut.

The Armalite chattered as Jan returned fire. "I knocked out part of his windshield, but he's ducked under my shooting angle!" she yelled.

"Keep at him! Try to keep him ducked down so he can't see to drive!" Traveler shouted over his shoulder.

The ravine was scallop-edged, and the edges were crumbling, several times giving way when he got too near them. He jerked the wheel sharply to the right—and suddenly they'd come to the end.

An immense boulder blocked their path. The only escape was obvious. On foot.

"Jan, come up here and get out of the van! Its angled so he can't hit you if you get out on the right side! Hurry!"

"Forget it," she said. "I get out when you get out."

He swore. He had no intention of leaving the Meat Wagon and running.

The semi was bearing down on them. Twenty feet behind. Ten, now . . .

Traveler swung hard to the left and stepped on the gas. The Meat Wagon ran itself off the edge of the ravine. For a moment its front wheels spun in space, then it tilted downward. The incline wasn't perpendicular. It was at about a 70-degree angle. But the incline was steep enough to make him feel like he was diving headfirst into death.

He fought panic as they pitched down the walls of the ravine, the floor of the dry wash rushing up at them. There were boulders below, but there was a hump of alluvial dirt, too. He turned the wheel slightly that way—all this in a split second—careful not to turn too much. The wheels had to be relatively straight or the van would skid out of control.

The Meat Wagon shot downward, the rocks seemed to fling themselves up at him—and then the wheels found purchase on the wall of the ravine and angled the van toward the open space. The Meat Wagon came to rest with a *whuff*ing jounce against the hump of earth, more or less horizontal.

Jan was picking herself up. She looked out the rear firing slit.

"The bastard's up there on the edge, trying to decide what to do," she said. "He'll never— No! I don't believe it!"

Traveler looked in the side mirror. The semi was tipping over the edge.

"Son of a bitch!" Traveler burst out.

He backed the van up and it stopped, beginning to spin in place. The ground was too soft. The wheels weren't gripping.

And the big semi was tipping over the edge, coming down. . . . The crazy guy's coming down on top of us! Traveler thought.

He jerked the wheel desperately first one way, then the other, trying to dig the wheels in for purchase. He hit the gas again, and the van lurched backward and to one side. The semitruck came down the slope like a monstrous mailed fist—and smashed into the spot they'd occupied

80

half a second before. Its weight had brought it down too fast: It tipped over onto its top, growled, and spun its wheels angrily. The engine died and the semi rocked there for a moment like a turtle turned on its back. And then— *thud*—fell over onto its right side.

Traveler straightened the van out in the dry wash and moved it behind a ridge of earth. He wondered if he'd ever get it out of the gulley again.

He reached behind the seat, grabbed up the heavy assault rifle, and got out. Jan followed, carrying the Armalite. They moved cautiously around the bank of yellow dirt and scree to the semi's crash site.

The semi was lying on its side, ticking, a thin gray vapor rising from its exhaust pipe. Traveler thought of a Ray Harryhausen dinosaur he'd seen on the late show as a boy, a tyrannosaurus dying in a city street, lying on its side, now and then thrashing its tail, its eyes glazing. . . .

The door was open on the upper side of the overturned cab. Maybe the guy had already climbed out. Maybe . . .

Traveler turned and saw a big black man—a brown man, really—atop a boulder, just above him. The man had a knife in his hand. He crouched, preparing to leap at them. His eyes were . . . dead.

Jan swung the Armalite around and popped it to her shoulder.

She looked at Traveler in amazement when he slapped it down. "Don't shoot!" Traveler said. "He's—"

He didn't get any more out, because the guy had leapt, was smashing down on him, the knife flashing.

Traveler was knocked flat on his back, the Heckler & Koch flying from his grasp. The wind knocked out of him. The black guy was astraddle him, knees pinning Traveler's arms, the knife raised to slash. The gaunt black face stared down at him, expressionless as a slaughterhouse hog-killer.

"Orwell!" he shouted. "Dammit, Orwell, it's me! It's Paxton! I'm your buddy!"

The hand holding the knife froze, the point of the blade stopping three inches over Traveler's windpipe.

The black man's face was contorted with some inner struggle. Then his eyes cleared, and he shook himself. He looked at Traveler.

"Puh . . . Paxton?"

"Yeah. Now get the fuck off me!"

Moving awkwardly, as if finding the operation of his body strange, as if someone else had been operating it for him till this moment, Orwell climbed off him and sheathed the knife at his belt. He wore old ripped jeans and a long brown leather coat, an old Second Chance vest showing beneath the coat.

He swayed. Blood trickled from a cut on his forehead, sustained in the crash.

He looked around dazedly. "What . . .?"

Traveler got to his feet. He felt like he'd been through a wringer. He dusted himself off and said, "Orwell, you're crazy. . . ."

Orwell looked at Traveler. "That really you, man?"

"It's me. You trying to pirate my van?"

"I—guess I must've been. But . . . I seem to remember driving off a cliff. And that ain't something I'm ready to do in the regular line of work." He rubbed his head. "Ooh, big mother of a headache."

Jan was looking back and forth between the two men. "Where you know him from?" she asked Traveler.

"Army. Long Range Recon Patrol, Delta Force—the crazies brigade. We were partners. We got hit at the same time with the neurotoxin. We all flipped out, and I lost track of them after that."

"But"—she shook her head—"the coincidence . . .!"

Traveler snorted. "It's no coincidence. The Black Rider

set this up. He reads minds. He knew about Orwell and Hill and Margolin. He happened to know Orwell was alive. He brought us together this way, I figure, so I'd be killed by a friend. That suits the Rider, that kind of vengeance. The more twisted the better.''

Orwell was staring at him. "The Rider . . . yeah, I remember. He did something to me. Took hold of me. Then all I could think about was killing the guy they call . . ." He grinned. "So *you're* Traveler! I heard about you before! And all the time it was Kiel Paxton!''

Jan was smiling. "Kiel? No wonder you changed your name!''

"That isn't why," Traveler said softly.

Orwell was getting his composure back. "Yo, man!" He clapped Traveler on the shoulders. "Man! Paxton! You're alive!''

Traveler grinned at him, then the grin faded. "The nerve gas, man. The neurotoxin. How'd you . . . ?''

"It was rough, man." Orwell sank onto a rock, getting his breath. "I guess I was out of it for months. I was in a fallout shelter. Then I snapped out of it long enough to steal a radiation suit and get out of that hole. I been wandering . . . I guess I wasn't sane for about five, six years. I still get fits of paranoia. And the . . . it's hard to describe. Like I can see and hear too much. And I can feel things that I can't see. Feel people when they're behind me, even. It makes you buggy. I got to get real stoned on something. Booze or something. I got a connection for opium . . . that helps . . .''

"But in a lot of ways it's worn off, right?" Jan asked, glancing at Traveler.

"Sure," Orwell told her. "I'm . . . functional. Say, you the one that shot out my windshield?''

"Yeah. My name's Jan. Before you ask, my tribe's Cheyenne. Traveler and I are working together.''

"Nice to meetcha. Even if you did almost blow my head off." He glanced over his shoulder at the semi, grimaced, and looked away from it. "Shit. That machine was all I had." His mouth went grim. "That Black Rider's ass is grass."

Traveler nodded. "We'll get him. We both owe him. But there's somebody else we owe first. The guy that fed us to the El Hiagurans. Vallone. He set us up and now his bills have come due."

Orwell nodded. "That's the way I figure it, too."

"I know where Vallone is."

Orwell looked keenly interested. "Yeah?"

"Still in the service. Guess he 're-ups' every year." They laughed. "He's in charge of external operations out of Base Zero. He's the top Glory Boy, I hear. I'm gonna go in after him—Jan has a way we can get in. Along the way, we'll get her brother out of stir, let loose the other prisoners, and in general do our best to inconvenience those sons of bitches who pushed the world into this burnt-out radioactive shit pile. We'll do 'em good."

"I'm coming along, man."

"That's what I wanted to hear," Traveler said, nodding. "Now let's see if we can get my van out of this hole."

# 10

## The Flesh Traders

"So where's the backup team you mentioned?" Orwell asked as he replaced the vial of antitoxin in the minifridge. "Say, I do feel better. I was getting all shaky. The stuff works. . . ."

"Eight men from my tribe," Jan said. "They're coming cross-country on horseback, meeting us near the base. Then we get the lay of the place and work up a plan. But first we stop in Drift, make our army connections, bluff our way in."

"Do we hit Vallone in Drift?" Orwell asked. He was sitting on a gun case in the back. The van was humming smoothly down the highway again, which was a relief after all the gruelling overland work they'd had to do, the pushing and levering and clearing of rocks to get the van out of the dry wash and onto the road.

"Vallone doesn't work out of the depot in Drift," she said. "There's a scumbag named Wentworth there now. . . ."

"What's this?" Traveler asked. He was at the wheel, one hand hovering near the button that fired his overhead machine guns.

There was a roadblock up ahead.

"It's okay," Jan said. She was in the passenger seat.

"That's the Drift 'tollbooth.' Gotta bribe 'em. If you don't have gold you got to haggle over supplies."

Traveler reached to an inside pocket of his flak jacket, pulled out a leather bag, and took a gram of pure gold from it. That was an established unit of exchange.

"You don't have to give 'em so much," she said.

"Hoping to buy a friend to cover my ass," he explained.

They pulled up at the crude wooden roadblock. It was made of oil drums with boards chained onto them. There was a kind of corral gate in the middle, closed now. Eight men, looking like heavily armed hobos, were perched on the roadblock at various places, hats pulled low to give them a little protection against the late afternoon sun.

Traveler drew the .45, keeping it in sight in his left hand but pointed upward.

A potbellied man with only three yellowed teeth left in his mouth came to the van's driver's side window. Traveler opened it just enough.

The man pushed a floppy leather hat back on his head and scratched his verminous red beard as he looked through the windshield, checking them out.

He seemed to recognize Jan. He shouted over his shoulder at the others, "It's that Injun broad! She got herself two new boyfriends."

"What's the toll?" Traveler asked.

"For three people, fren', a half-gram of gold or what we consider to be equal in trade goods such as—"

"Never mind. Here." He passed a lump of gold to the man. The gatekeeper held the gold up in the light, scrutinizing it closely.

"Yeah, that's the stuff."

"Half is for you. Just a friendly gesture."

"Yeah? What's your name, fren'?"

"I'm Traveler."

The man took a step back. "Now we don't want no trouble—"

Orwell laughed. "Looks like your rep preceded you, man."

Traveler said, "So what's *your* name, gatekeeper?"

"Huh, me? They call me Leatherhead."

"Leatherhead, huh? Listen—you see the Black Rider around?"

Leatherhead swallowed. He looked over his shoulder before answering. In a whisper: "Yeah. Passed through. Came and went."

"You see him again, get me word, and you'll have a good friend. And anybody else who asks about me or this van. Okay?"

Leatherhead looked at the gold in his hand. "Sure. But listen—no trouble, huh? We try to discourage fighting in Drift. Because when there's fighting," he explained, "people get killed."

"Good policy. We don't mess with anybody who doesn't mess with us." After a moment he added, "If they *do* mess with us, though, they get messed up *good*!"

Leatherhead grinned, and it wasn't a pretty sight.

He turned to the others and shouted, "Let 'em on through!"

The gate rolled away, and the van rolled through.

There were only four streets in Drift but scores of small twisted alleys, warrens, and rooftop walkways between the bigger buildings. None of the buildings were bigger than two stories. Most were ramshackle huts, shacks, sheds, and a great many people lived in their cars, whether or not the cars were operational.

Drift had been built—or, rather, had accumulated—over the ruins of a small crossroads town that had been called Welton Corners. None of the original inhabitants remained, having been killed by a roadrat horde a decade earlier. Then Marshal Dillon had come and opened a trading depot. His name was Andrew Dillon, but when he got to be the local peacekeeper—meaning he and his eight men shot anybody who caused trouble—they started calling him "Marshal." After a while he even took to wearing a tin badge on his chest, cadged from some trash heap. It had once been a children's toy. But the Colt .45 he packed was no toy, and neither were the sawed-off shotguns his men carried. He demanded heavy taxes from anybody who stayed in Drift, so you didn't stay there long if you didn't earn something, some way, or if you didn't have something valuable stashed away. About half the people there were itinerant, coming in to trade or to get some pussy at the slime pit that passed for a whorehouse.

Jan explained all this to Traveler as they looked for someplace to park the van, concluding, "There's only four Glory Boys at the army trading depot here. Dillon won't let them bring any more in. Won't let the army come near the town—he's afraid they'd try to take it over. They probably will, sooner or later. I guess right now they find Drift useful as it is. And Drift's pretty well fortified. Dillon's got eight deputies, but there are maybe five hundred men who'd defend the place if the army tried to move in. And Dillon's got some antitank guns, some light artillery, stuff stolen from National Guard armories. The army knows that too."

They found a spot vacant in a swatch of asphalt, once part of a Welton Corners parking lot. Only the Welton Corners Methodist Church remained standing of the old town, and Dillon used that for his HQ.

Traveler turned off the Meat Wagon and got out carrying the assault rifle.

After Jan and Orwell got out—Orwell carrying a Thompson SMG he'd had in his semi—Traveler set the van's booby traps to protect it while he was away.

Traveler looked around. The sunlight glanced from tin roofs and stung his eyes. The smell assaulted his nostrils. The layout of the place offended his sense of orderliness. It looked like a junkyard with a lot of people mixed in with the junk. The street to his left was crammed with cars and hulks of cars, and cars that had been cut away and made into horsedrawn carts. Horses were tied up here and there. Thievery was rampant in Drift and usually a man there had a partner who watched his stuff while he went about his business; then he came back, and his friend went on his errands while the first man watched the car or the horses or the cart filled with salvage.

There was a row of outhouses on a dirt road to one side. Trash was piled up in every unused nook. But someone was always picking through the trash, looking for something useful.

Sullen, envious men glared at them. They were envious because, despite the new gouges on the side, the Meat Wagon was a beautiful machine. And because they had automatic weapons. And because there was a girl with Traveler. To them, Traveler was like a feudal lord riding through a peasant hamlet, ostentatious with his riches.

Traveler took a pair of steel-framed dark glasses from his shirt pocket to cut the glare and soften the impact of seeing so many people. He put them on, and they started toward the depot.

Traveler stopped when something above him barked and snarled warningly. He looked up. A feral canine face was peering over the eave of a wooden shack, ten feet overhead.

"What is *that*?" he blurted.

Orwell laughed. "You ain't seen those things? That's a climbing dog. Half cat, sort of. Big as a damned German

89

shepherd. A mutant. This town is infested with 'em. Some people keep 'em for pets. But they're mean little fuckers.''

Traveler watched as another dog—with claws rather like a marsupial's—ran up the side of the shack, clawing its way up like a cat chased up a tree.

"Traveler?" Jan said, tugging at his shirt sleeve.

"Yeah?"

"Someone back there's messing around with the Meat Wagon.''

He turned. He bent and could see, under the van, someone's feet—someone on the far side of the van bending to unscrew the lug nuts from the wheels. Stealing his tires.

They were joined by a second pair of feet. Then a third.

Traveler and Orwell looked at one another. Orwell pointed to the front of the van. Traveler nodded and moved toward the rear.

He crouched and peered around the fender. Two grizzled, big-shouldered guys with bushy beards were working at his front tires. Each one carried a monkey wrench. A third bearded guy with a dirty white jacket two sizes too small for him was working on the rear wheels. A group of Drift loafers were watching from across the street. Traveler decided to make an example. He set the gun aside, remembering that Marshal Dillon didn't like "promiscuous gunfire" in the streets, and approached the two men. He stood behind them.

He cleared this throat.

The two men straightened with a jerk and whirled to face him. They both stood a good six inches taller, each outweighing him by at least fifty pounds.

"Put the nuts back on that wheel," Traveler said, loudly enough so the loafers across the street could hear him.

The bigger of the two men laughed and rushed him, wrench uplifted.

Traveler waited till the wrench was flashing down at him. Then he grabbed the man's wrist, twisted, stepped under, and performed a perfect judo flip. The big man's momentum carried him over onto his back—and as he fell, Traveler changed the leverage on the arm he held so that it would be wrenched out of its socket by the fall. The big man struck the ground, screaming at the pain as his arm was jerked from its socket. The other man was coming on at the same moment his friend hit the ground. Traveler moved with blur-swiftness, sidestepping, grabbing up the wrench and clouting the second thug hard on the side of the head as he passed. *Whump!* The second big man pitched flat on his face, a felled ox.

Traveler turned to see Orwell take on the other one.

Orwell and the guy in the white jacket were circling one another. The white-jacket held a big knife; Orwell had nothing. Orwell laughed and said, ''Come on, man, you got the knife, don't be such a wimp!''

The guy rushed him. In a LURP move so fast it was a flash, Orwell disarmed the guy, broke his wrist, then his elbow, then kicked him so he fell headfirst into the Meat Wagon's right rear fender. He lay still after that.

''Hey, watch out, Orwell, you're gonna mess up my paint job bouncing these jerks off it!'' Traveler said.

''Look out, man!'' Orwell shouted.

Traveler ducked. A knife flashed past his ear. The man whose arm he'd dislocated was coming after him, a knife in his good hand, the other arm hanging like dead meat.

Traveler kicked out, caught the swollen arm hard just below the shoulder with the toe of his boot. The man howled and staggered.

Traveler was tired of the game. He grabbed up his rifle—but by the barrel. He swung it like a baseball bat when the batter is hooking the bat up to catch a ball coming in low, and connected with the bearded brute's nose, so that blood splashed and cartilage ripped. The man fell over on his ass. Traveler followed up with a neat kick to the point of the big man's chin—he had to guess at the chin's whereabouts since it was hidden in so much foliage, but he guessed accurately, the boot connected, and the big man flopped over, out cold.

Traveler glanced at the loafers across the street. They were all careful to make their expressions neutral or friendly. One of them even made a thumb's-up gesture.

Jan was standing to one side, the Armalite ready, in case he should need backing up.

"You guys through playing cowboys, or can we go and get some work done now?" she said with mock-weariness.

Orwell grinned at Traveler. "Now I know who wears the pants."

"Screw you," Traveler said. "We're just work—" He broke off. There were four men with sawed-off shotguns coming toward them from across the street. Traveler reversed the Heckler and Koch, held it ready.

They wore black cowboy hats and leather stars pinned to their black leather jackets. On each star someone had burned the word, *Deputy*.

They stopped three paces from Traveler, the shotguns raised.

"Drop the rifles," one of them said. "No one but the deputies carry guns in this town."

Traveler had had a long day, and he was fed up.

"Fuck off," he said. "You want this gun, you got to kill me for it."

# 11

## Glory Boys

The one who'd demanded the guns looked genuinely surprised. He wasn't used to having his sawed-off shotguns argued with.

He was a tall, angular man, lean and squinty, red-faced and radiating suspicion about everything. Orwell, carrying the Thompson now, stepped up beside Traveler to back him up, though he gave him a sidelong look that said, "You're still crazy!"

Jan flanked Traveler on the other side, the Armalite ready. The three of them spread out so one shot couldn't hit all three—even a shot from one of these scatter-guns.

"We got to impound those guns," the gawky deputy said. "Them's the rules."

"You send a man to the marshal," Traveler said. "Tell him these guns are more precious to me than gold. Tell him I don't mess with anybody who doesn't mess with me. Tell him Traveler sent the message."

"Traveler, huh? I guess I'm supposed to be impressed. But I don't think I'm gonna be impressed by a man cut in half by a load of buckshot. He's just dead meat, that man."

"And what about a man who's cut to ribbons by three automatic weapons? Maybe we'd do each other if it came

93

to shooting. But you wouldn't come out of it alive, either,'' Traveler pointed out calmly.

The man's face twitched. His fingers tightened on the shotgun.

Traveler flicked the HK's safety off.

And then the deputy seemed to sag inside his clothing. He spoke to a short, stubby man beside him. "Go get the marshal. Tell him what this guy said.''

The little man trotted off. They waited for about seven minutes, the sun and the tension making sweat on their faces and necks. Three men in black cowboy hats staring at three very strange strangers.

Then Marshal Dillon came out of the church down the street and came striding down the middle of the road.

He was an immense, bearlike man with a forked beard and tufted eyebrows. A tin star flashed on his leather vest. He wore a black cowboy hat from which waved a long red feather. A climbing dog ran in circles about his feet. Now and then he'd kick at it, catching it in the ribs. It would slink away, whining, and then come back to get in his way again.

He and the stubby deputy walked up to the face-off. Dillon was carrying only a .45 revolver strapped to his blue-jeaned hip.

"You're smaller'n I thought you'd be,'' he said, seeing Traveler. "What I heard about you . . .'' He shrugged. He nodded toward the fallen men. "You put them down?''

"Uh-huh. Me and Orwell here,'' Traveler said.

"Hiya, Marshal,'' Orwell said, smiling coolly. He had the Thompson pointed at Dillon's gut.

"Yeah,'' Dillon said, "I know Orwell here. We hired him to truck some stuff for us. Orwell's okay. But maybe he got into some bad company. . . . So you think you're gonna keep those guns.''

94

"I know I am. I'm going to keep 'em long as I'm alive," Traveler said with complete conviction.

Dillon sighed. "But you see—that sets a bad example. Gives me a dilemma. I don't want you shooting up my deputies, but . . . I don't want my rules broken. Things are hard enough to keep in order here. . . . Now, wait. I got me an idea." He turned to the deputies, and as they gaped in dismay, unpinned three leather stars from three vests. He tossed them to Orwell. "You and your buddy put those on. And the girl, dammit. Then you're deputies while you're here. I appoint you." He shouted up and down the street. "You all hear? These people are my deputies!" He turned back to Traveler. "So you can keep your guns. Okay? But you turn over the badges when you leave— which should be as soon as possible."

Traveler shrugged. What the hell.

He let Orwell pin the badge on him.

One of the deputies, who were now badgeless, complained, "But, Sheriff, we need them badges to keep order or else people laugh in our faces!"

"They laugh, anyway," Dillon said. "Come on, children, back to the office. I'll have Billy make you some more. All the children got to have their badges." The deputies followed him down the street.

Orwell shook his head and sighed. "Traveler, you crazy."

"I don't go without a weapon, not anywhere," Traveler said. "And I'm not going to leave the van unguarded. . . ."

Two of the deputies returned. As an afterthought, Dillon had sent them to haul away the men who'd tried to steal Traveler's wheels. They hauled the unconscious men in a horse-drawn cart to Drift's jail.

"I'll stay with the Meat Wagon," Orwell said. "You don't need me, anyway. And I'll put the damn lugs back on. . . ."

"Thanks." Traveler and Jan crossed the street, walking

on a wooden sidewalk beside crazily leaning shanties and open-air booths selling odds and ends of food.

At the far end of the street they came to an old barn with two men stationed at the entrance. That was the trading depot.

"Let me do the talking," Jan said.

Traveler nodded and followed her in.

There were heavy iron doors and bars installed to protect the old barn. It was stifling hot inside, the air close with the reek of human sweat and desperation. To the right was a steel-framed pen, a cage made from hurricane-fence wire. Men and women were packed into it. At least forty.

There was room for only thirty.

Traveler saw someone he recognized, pressed to the wire. Junie Kettering, the red-haired horsey-faced girl from Kettering's Survivalist camp. He ignored the glares of the Glory Boy guards posted on either side of the trading table and walked up to the cage.

"What happened?" he asked her.

She stared bitterly at him. "Big horde of roadrats. Come and caught us by surprise. We was having a wedding party. I was getting married." She broke off, sobbing. "Everybody was drunk. And then the roadrats come and . . ." She shrugged. "There ain't there no one left alive but me. In the whole camp. They shot my husband, raped and killed all the girls. By the time they was done with the others, they found me hiding under a shed. . . ."

"So you didn't get raped?"

"No." She sounded vaguely disappointed. "They ran into a bunch of Glory Boys when they were taking me out to the roadrat camp. The Glory Boys shot 'em up. Took me for a slave."

"Kettering's dead?"

She nodded. "What about—?"

"They're dead, too. Joe and Harry and Burt and Morris."

He didn't feel like going into detail about that.

He turned on his heel and went to the trading table, a big slab of wood on two sawhorses. There was a gram scale on it, and a record book. A thin, pale man in a U.S. Army uniform, a captain, frowned up at Traveler and Jan, who'd waited for him just inside the door.

"How much for the redhead?" Traveler said.

The man's frown deepened. His nametag said WENTWORTH. "We hadn't planned to sell her. She was earmarked for the labs."

"Meaning your weapons researchers are going to try out some new toys on her."

Wentworth shrugged.

Traveler persisted. "How much?"

"One gram of gold."

Traveler winced. But he found his pouch, extracted the gold, and laid it on the table. Wentworth handed it to a man standing beside him. The man bit it, scrutinized it, and nodded. Wentworth took the gold back and slipped it into a shirt pocket. The man looked as if he were going to protest this but thought better of it. Wentworth scribbled in the record book, then took a receipt book from his shirt pocket, made out a receipt—after getting the prisoner's number, which was stamped on a metal wristband—and handed it to Traveler.

They let the girl out. She went meekly to stand behind him.

Jan was looking at Traveler oddly. He pretended not to notice.

Other women in the cage shouted at him, "How about it, honey. I'd do you good! They'd give you a deal on me, ask 'em! Come on, buy me out of here!"

Traveler forced himself to ignore them.

Wentworth was looking at Jan. "I've seen you before. . . ."

"I was here negotiating for the release of my brother."

"Oh, yes. The Indian boy . . ." Wentworth's eyes lit up. "The storage dump! You're ready to give us the location?"

She shook her head. "Not till we get an interview with Major Vallone. And I want to see my brother, see that he's alive. I figure we could do both the same day. You send word ahead, we go out to wherever he's being kept, we see Martin, and then negotiate the deal with Vallone."

The Glory Boy guards chuckled at her impudence. They wore a mix of U.S. Army issue and denim or leather. Each one had a red-white-and-blue cloth tied around his arm or ankle. They carried M16s.

They'd been staring at the automatic weapons Traveler and Jan carried, and they kept their M16s high, pointed in Traveler's general direction if not exactly aimed. He got the message.

He didn't make any quick moves.

Looking calmly at her, Wentworth said. "You know, we don't want any trouble with the Indians. But—we could always just take you. And torture the information out of you."

"You could if I had it. I don't know where the place is. Only my father and one other know. They are hidden in the hills—you'd never find them. Even if you located my father, you'd have to fight through the whole tribe to get to him. I guarantee you'd have heavy losses. Hand over my brother and you'll have the location."

"Give us the location and you'll have your brother."

Thirty seconds of silent impasse. Then she shrugged.

She said, "Okay. If I can see him—and get a promise, face-to-face, from Major Vallone."

Wentworth pursed his lips. "I'll radio the major for instructions. Come back in two hours."

He bent over the record book. They were dismissed. Traveler and Jan turned to walk out of the barn, both feeling relieved to get away from there. Prisoners howled at them from the cage. One of the guards pulled a broken-off antenna aerial from his belt, telescoped it out, and began whipping at the hands imploring through the cage wire. "Shut up, you fucking animals!" he bellowed.

Traveler's jaw muscles worked. He started toward the guard.

Jan took Traveler firmly by the arm and whispered, "You'll blow the mission."

Reluctantly, he turned away and they went out into the sunlight.

It was easing into twilight. The shadows were long on the crazy-quilt street. The air was raucous with the noises of cars, horses, men laughing, hammers banging as someone insulated a shed with tin-can lids.

The noise seemed to get louder and louder. Traveler felt the press of people around him as a psychic abrasion. He started back to the van, Jan beside him. He was aware of someone trotting after him.

He stopped and turned, remembering. Junie looked hopefully at him. He dug another half-gram of gold from his bag and pressed it into her palm. "Take this. You're free now. Beat it."

She looked at him pleadingly. "You don't want me? What'd you buy me for, then?"

Jan looked at him, too, to see what his answer would be.

He said, "I took on a job for your dad. I didn't follow it through. In fact, I went over to your opposition. I joined the people your old man sent me out after. But I figure I owe you people something—you gave me the car and the food and fuel to go after my van. So I bought your freedom to discharge that debt. You're free to go.''

Jan was smiling ever so slightly. "Hey, you're not such a tough guy, Mr. T.''

"I try to stay human, that's all.''

"But look"—Junie whined, following him again as they walked to the van—"look at how people are checking me out here. They'll just grab me and sell me again. Or worse. I'm not a fighter. I'm a housemaker. I can't defend myself. I haven't got a gun. I—''

"All right, all right!'' Traveler said, turning angrily on her. "So shut up! I'll—'' He let out a long breath. The place was getting to him. Grinding at him with its scents, sounds, the presence of people. "I'll take care of you till we can get to somewhere safer. Maybe we can set you up with another colony. Just shut up.''

Back at the Meat Wagon, Orwell was sitting on a box in a ten-by-ten-foot square painted recently in white on the asphalt of the cracked parking lot.

"What's this?'' Traveler asked.

"That's our little home for tonight,'' Orwell said, lighting a hand-rolled cigarette. "Dillon's men came back and collected 'Overnight Taxes' from me and painted out this square. It means we're allowed to camp in here. Light a fire in here and cook if we want. I bought some kindling from an old man . . . I guess I could've gathered it myself, but he needed a little food. . . .'' He shrugged and looked embarrassed.

"You're a good-hearted man,'' Junie said. "What's your name?''

Orwell looked at her with interest. "I'm Joe Orwell. Who's she, Paxton?''

Traveler sighed. "I'll let her explain it. I'm going in the van for a while.''

100

"It's getting dark," Junie said. "I'll build a fire. You got any food? I can cook you a little something. . . . "

"Well, I got a gunnysack of tinned stuff I brought from my truck," Orwell said.

"What happened to your truck?"

"That's a long story. Tell me yours first, pretty lady."

"Do you—really think I'm pretty?"

"Cleaned up, you would be. I always fancied red hair."

Traveler rolled his eyes back and reached under the van door to unlatch the booby trap. Then he got in and climbed in back. He drank half a vial of antitoxin and felt a little better.

He lay on the cot, staring at the ceiling. It was good to see Orwell. If he had survived, maybe Hill and Margolin were alive somewhere. Knife Wind's tribe seemed to have it together. Maybe there was hope for humanity. Not much. But maybe just a little. And there was Jan. . . .

She climbed in, said, "Uh—can I get some water?"

"Sure."

She climbed into the back and found a canteen. She took a long swig, put it aside. "Mind if I sit down?"

"Go ahead."

She sat on the edge of the cot. "Listen, why didn't you shoot me that day? I mean, why'd you shoot down the guys you were with?"

"I wasn't really with 'em. I was just putting up with 'em. They're scum, no better than roadrats. And—I guess I figured you took my van for the sake of your tribe's survival."

"That raid was a retaliation. The Survivalists hit us first."

"Yeah? I'm not surprised."

"But wasn't there another reason you didn't shoot me? Maybe because I wasn't armed. None of us were—we had

101

guns, but not in our hands. And we were two women and a boy.''

"Yeah. So what's the point?"

"The point is . . . you're not like the rest.''

He looked at her. "Maybe in some ways I'm worse.''

"I don't believe that. . . .'' She looked at him.

Outside it was getting dark. And noisier. Drift had the only "nightlife" for hundreds of miles around. Dirt-floor bars and whorehouses used generators to crank electricity into old stereos, blasting out rock music from scratchy records two decades old. Billy Idol's "Rebel Yell" was kicking sonic ass from the two-story shack next door. All that noise covered the sounds from within the van as Traveler and Jan made love.

It just happened, like spontaneous combustion.

One moment she was looking into his eyes, the next they were locked in an embrace, lips grinding together, tongues moiling, hips grinding on hips. She was lean and strong, boa-constrictor lithe against him, hot with suppressed sexuality now bubbling free.

Somehow in the darkness they got undressed, and then they were skin on skin. His toxified nerves were still a bit sensitive, but he put that sensitivity to good use this time, feeling every square inch of her smooth copper skin, her hard ass under his hands, her neat little breasts, hard nipples nosing eagerly at his chest. She drew him into her and pulled him on top, urged his hips into machine-gun rapidity. . . .

The first two times they made it, they did it hot and fast, a frantic release of tension. The third time it was slow and luxurious and exploratory, and they seemed to be floating away together on gently rocking waves of their mutual undulation. . . .

Finally exhausted, they dozed in each other's arms.

Then she sat bolt upright. "The traders! We got to go see 'em!"

He groaned and reached for his pants, his boots, and his gun.

Feeling oddly displaced, wishing it had happened at a better time, they got dressed and climbed outside. Orwell and Junie were sitting close together beside a fire. Orwell was sopping up gravy from a metal plate with bread. "This little lady can cook!" he crowed. "Try it, man!"

"No time. Watch the van, we'll be back."

"Sure, man . . . uh, say, Kiel, man—okay with you if we guard the Meat Wagon from *inside* it?"

"Sure. Go ahead."

"Thanks, man, don't worry about a thing, we—"

Junie already had him by the wrist, dragging him toward the van. "Didn't you hear him? He said go ahead! Come on!"

"Talk about who wears the pants," Traveler muttered.

He and Jan went to the trading depot. Torches lit the interior, making it look like an inquisition chamber, with high, flickering shadows and yellow light on the faces of the men at the table. And on the prisoners waiting to one side.

Two guys wearing long riding coats and droopy-brimmed hats had an old man between them, beside the trading table. A guard was clipping a metal bracelet on the old man's wrist. He'd just been sold for "experiments."

"You call yourself U.S. Army!" the old man shouted. "I was in the army! I was a sergeant in Nam! I got me a Silver Star! I'm a U.S. citizen and you're buying and selling U.S. citizens, and you pretend you're the damned government!"

"All citizens were given five years to report to the government office at Base Zero. We sent it out by radio and postered it. Anyone who didn't report is an outlaw,

103

and all outlaws are impounded for labor-force work," Wentworth said blandly. A recital.

"Government office! I didn't know there was any government office! We didn't have a radio. I didn't see any posters. Damn you! And damn Frayling!" the old man shrieked.

Traveler smiled.

The Glory Boys, fanatically loyal to President Frayling, weren't smiling. They beat the old man about the head till he sagged, out cold, and dumped him in the cage.

"You guys are real heroes," Traveler said, looking at the Glory Boys.

The bigger of the two guards turned toward Traveler. "What you say?"

"He didn't say anything," Jan said, stepping up to the table. "We're here for business. Well, Wentworth?"

Wentworth nodded. "The major says yes. Tomorrow morning you ride with us to the detention camp near Base Zero. You see your brother, then we go to Major Vallone's office. Report here at one hour past dawn."

She nodded curtly and they turned and walked out.

Outside she said, "Traveler, I know how you feel about slavery. I feel the same way. But we've got to play along till the time's right. We've got to be actors."

He nodded. "You're right."

She took his hand, squeezed it, then dropped it and walked by his side the way a male companion would. She wasn't one for public displays of emotion. That was okay with him.

They passed a torchlit yard, stopped on the far side of it to look at a crowd.

The crowd had gathered in a multilayered semicircle behind three deputies who were lined up and standing at attention. Marshal Dillon stood to one side. At the other end of the yard was a bullet-pocked crust of a brick wall,

104

like something left from the Alamo. The three would-be tire thieves Traveler and Orwell had knocked out were now standing up against that wall, blindfolded.

A man in a dented top hat and overalls was walking briskly through the crowd shouting, "Place yer bets!" stopping now and then to collect betting gold and a name.

Traveler heard someone say, "I'm betting two out of three die first."

A man replied, "You kidding? These deputies can't shoot for shit. It'll take 'em three tries to kill 'em all. I'm betting three trics for all three men."

Traveler glanced at Jan. She seemed interested, as if she were tempted to bet. There is a touch of cat-playing-with-mouse cruelty in some Indians.

Someone nudged Traveler's arm. He whirled, stepping back, gun raised.

"Take it easy, fren'!" It was Leatherhead. He grinned, and as Traveler lowered the gun, he stepped in to whisper, "Don't let on you heard this from me. But there's a special shooter that Black Rider hired. He's here to kill you. And he's watching you from across the street, right now."

# 12

## The Tall Man

"Don't turn and look at him while I'm talking to you," Leatherhead whispered. "Pretend you're taking a bet with me. Yeah. Wait a minute before turning—he's just watching you right now. Wearing a black leather cap. Tall guy."

Traveler nodded. Leatherhead trotted away and faded into the crowd.

Traveler counted to sixty. He turned, as if to survey the street out of curiosity. Then he saw the man. The killer. At the same moment Traveler laid eyes on the guy, the firing squad in the execution yard pulled their triggers. A triple flash from the muzzles, howls of glee from the crowd. Someone yelled, "Shit they *all* still alive! You guys can't shoot for nothing!"

Traveler and the Tall Man looked at each other.

Each man had heard about the other.

The Tall Man was a hit artist who worked for anyone who paid enough. He wore a black leather coat that hung down past his knees and a black leather biker's cap. His glasses were red-tinted, and the lenses were oddly thick— and then Traveler recognized them as night-vision goggles.

The Tall Man was thin, hawk-nosed, hollow-cheeked, and a little stooped. His hands were long and pale. Traveler could see no weapons on him. But from what Traveler had heard, the guy could kill with almost anything. It was said he specialized in rifles, though—long-range hits. He was rumored to have been a KGB hit man who'd been stranded in the States by the war. It was also that he was so confident of a kill that once he'd set it up, he went after it with only a single bullet in his gun. And supposedly he'd never failed.

The two men looked at one another. And then Traveler turned away. He couldn't attack the man here, with the sheriff nearby.

"Was that the guy in the long coat?" Jan asked softly as they stepped over drunks and ducked under the slathering muzzles of climbing dogs hanging from roof overhangs.

Traveler nodded.

"Traveler, what if we get Dillon to jail him. Just to prevent trouble. Dillon might do it."

"I doubt it. Dillon wouldn't want to cross the Black Rider. Anyway, that would only be a temporary solution. Unfinished business."

"So you're gonna be the macho guy and have it out with him."

He looked sharply at her. "You're starting to sound like a wife."

That shut her up.

When they'd reached the van, she said, "Let's give Junie and Orwell some time together."

"Okay." Traveler approved. He wanted to be sure Junie was off his hands.

They crossed the street, stepping over various kinds of droppings, and entered a ramshackle two-story building that had been built of raw two-by-fours a few years earlier but somehow seemed as aged as a miner's shack from the nineteenth century. Over the door, crudely painted on a board, it said, BOB'S BAR AND GAL.

The place was about thirty-by-forty feet inside. At one end was a bar, a heavy board across two wooden barrels. Traveler noted a door that went out from behind the bar. Maybe the stairs to the cathouse on the second floor. A jug band, playing jugs, washboards, Jew's harp, and harmonica, was cranking out something like a tune against the left-hand wall. When they paused, Traveler could hear a rhythmic squeaking from the rickety ceiling overhead.

Traveler and Jan sat with their backs to the bar—on the side opposite the door to the stairs—facing the front door. They ordered two clay mugs of homemade brew. It was tepid but didn't taste bad.

There were about twenty men sitting at makeshift tables around the room. He saw no women. The men were gambling, drinking, staring sullenly at his guns. And at Jan. Some of them were talking about him. He didn't care.

He was thinking about the Tall Man.

The door to the back stairs opened, and a man came out, looking a little drained. Traveler glimpsed a line of men waiting on the stairs before the door closed. "How was she?" someone asked the man who'd come from upstairs.

"Ugly as a Bloat bitch, but not bad if you turn her facedown."

Traveler glanced at Jan. She was unaffected.

"Got a mess of beans and horsemeat cookin' up," the bartender announced. "Anybody hungry, we're taking tenth-gram chips or ammo for it."

Traveler turned to the stout, red-faced bartender. "Where'd you get the beans?"

"My old lady got 'em to grow, a secret place we got up in the hills. They're not tainted."

"Okay . . . how about two .22 rounds?"

"That'll do her."

Traveler took out the .22 rounds, which he had no use for except as barter, and passed them over. The bartender

108

ladled out two steel bowls of beans and meat in a thin, salty gravy. Jan looked at it critically. Then she nodded, "Yeah, it's horsemeat." They ate and finished their beers. The jug band cranked up again.

A fuzz-faced bruiser who could have been a football player if there were still such things as footballs teams, came reeling in. He stepped up to the bar. He wore a sleeveless denim jacket and a scarf over his head like a pirate. He showed a mouthful of big yellow teeth to Jan, grinning and looking her frankly up and down.

"You got to be paid for or you gonna give it to me for free?" the jock asked her.

"Neither," Traveler said. "You're not going to get it at all."

"I didn't say nothing to you," the jock said. Warningly.

"Doug," the bartender said, to the jock, "this fella is—"

"I don't give a fuck who he is!" Doug roared, breathing fumes on both Traveler and Jan. "A little wimp of a guy like him's got no right to a piece that fine!"

The jug band stopped playing, watching to see what would happen. Everyone else was watching. A lot of them were chuckling. Some were chuckling at Doug's expense, anticipating how it would end. Some at what Doug had said to Traveler.

Traveler simply waited.

Jan said, "Kid, you're unarmed. My friend and I here aren't. We're deputized."

Doug saw the guns for the first time, leaning against the bar. But he was drunk and obstinate. "So this guy's too much a pussy to fight for you without guns?"

He reached for her.

Traveler started to react. . . .

Jan said, "Let me do it this time."

Traveler smiled and shrugged. He relaxed.

The jock had his arm around her shoulders, was drawing her close with the other one. She made as if to snuggle in close to him, then made a lightning-swift movement with her right knee.

There was a squelching sound.

The jock turned white. He staggered back, holding his crotch. He tried to shout, but it came out a squeak. The bar roared with laughter.

He took about five long breaths, and the color returned to his face. Then he charged, roaring, at Jan.

She sidestepped and tripped him. He fell atop a table, flattening it to a heap of splinters. Men scrambled aside. He got to his knees, reached inside his jacket, whipped out a knife.

Jan turned and climbed quickly onto the bar. As the jock started to get to his feet, she jumped off, leaping straight up, coming down with both boot heels on the big lug's head. *Crack.* Then leaping clear.

He got a funny look on his face. His eyes crossed, and he fell flat, facedown, out like a switched-off light bulb.

Jan turned her back, leaned against the bar, and drank off half her beer. Traveler smiled and said, "I'm glad you're here to protect me."

The street was dark and nearly lifeless when they left the bar two hours later. Traveler paused in the doorway, wondering if the Tall Man would snipe him, here and now.

He knew he wouldn't, though. The Tall Man was nearby, all right. Traveler sensed him. But he wasn't going to shoot him down here. The Tall Man was waiting till he crossed the road.

Because the assassin was on the roof, directly overhead.

Traveler could feel him up there. An emanation of quiet predatory chill.

110

"What is it?" Jan whispered. "What's wrong?"

Traveler whispered, "Wait here till I'm out of sight. You'll hear a noise from the roof that'll be him moving out after me. It should be safe for you to cross the street then. I doubt he'd shoot at you, anyway. But just in case."

"What are you going to do?"

"Go after him. I can't leave it unfinished—or he'll finish it, sometime. So . . ." He shrugged.

"I'm going with you."

He looked at her and shook his head. She could read his expression in the light spilling out from the bar.

"But why not?"

"I can do it more efficiently alone. So could you, if you were in my place. I don't want to have to cover your ass, too. I've made up my mind. I'm going it alone."

"Okay."

A drunk stumbled past them from the bar and staggered out into the street.

Traveler could feel the assassin tense up on the roof overhead. And then relax as he realized the drunk wasn't Traveler.

The street's blocks of gray and black were splashed yellow by camp fires. A solitary deputy tramped down the street, patroling with a shotgun in his arms. He didn't see the killer in the well of shadow atop the roof. He strolled on, was lost from sight behind the confused array of parked vehicles.

Traveler handed the Heckler & Koch assault rifle to Jan. "I don't want to be encumbered by this. I've got the .45 and my throwing stars. And a knife. Wish I had the crossbow."

She took the rifle—now she had one under each arm— and . . . simply nodded. He could see her controlling the urge to kiss him good-bye.

He drew the .45 and moved to the left, into the shadows

111

of the narrow alley to one side of the bar, pressed close to the wooden wall.

Immediately, he heard the killer shifting on the roof.

Did the guy sense him, too?

Traveler crouched down, the gun outstretched, held in both hands, pointing it at a spot just above the black edge of the roof. The roof edge was dark against the blue-black of the night sky. A hunched man-shape blocked out the stars for a moment. Traveler aimed; the man-shape drew back. A faint scraping sound as the assassin dropped off the other side of the roof.

Now the man was on the ground. The bar was between them.

Traveler moved quickly down the alley. If the killer got there before Traveler, he'd be exposed, outlined against the open space and lights of the street.

The narrow alley, maybe four feet wide, angled off to the right, following the contours of an irregularly shaped hostelry. Someone had built the hostelry room by room, adding them one at a time as annexes, in no organized fashion. Lots of the buildings in Drift were that way, oddly shaped, and the general squeeze on the process of building things in Drift—forced by the necessity of having to keep them all within the safety of the outer walls—made new buildings shape themselves to conform to the old crooked ones. The effect was like jigsaw puzzle parts that hadn't been quite pressed together, irregular spaces left between parts that nearly interlocked.

Traveler followed one of these jigsaw paths to the right, looking for an ambush vantage.

It was dark. It stank: Not everyone used the outhouses. His eyes adjusted, and a little starlight filtered down. Chinks in some of the shacks let washed-out beams shine through at crooked intervals. But the light was like a few border guards overwhelmed by the army of shadows.

Traveler paused and listened. Scraps of conversation came softly from the buildings, muffled by the walls. He couldn't make out the words, but he could tell from the tone what the talking was about. Jeers. Challenges. Bawdy anecdotes. Whiny complaining. Conspiring.

He heard no footsteps in the narrow, crooked alley.

But he could feel a malevolent presence. A killer. About thirty feet away. Following.

To the left a shallow passage opened. A dead end. He stepped in it and looked around.

Traveler saw something waist-high and round, just a cylindrical darkness against the lighter shadow of a wall. He felt its edges. Flaky, cold, metallic. A rusty oil barrel.

Looking up, he saw a low roof edge, wood-shingled, above the barrel. He climbed atop the barrel, wincing at the slight metallic sound his boots made on it, and started to pull himself up onto the roof. He'd shoot from high ground. He got his elbows onto it, was going to hike his lower half up—and froze.

Two feral green-gold eyes glowed out of the darkness. Three feet away from his own eyes. They were looking at him.

A snarling. Starlight gleamed on bared teeth, pink gums.

A climbing dog. Judging by the size of those teeth, a big one.

The dog's snarling got louder and broke off into a bark. He heard its claws on the shingles. It was tensing to spring at him.

He had the gun in his right hand, but if he fired it, the Tall Man would know just where he was.

He lowered himself onto the barrel and felt hot dog breath on his cheek as the dog snapped at the place his face had been a moment before. Heard the click of its teeth.

A moment later he was crouching in the alley. He could feel someone approaching. It must be the Tall Man.

The dog was slathering up above. That would distract the Tall Man—hopefully.

Traveler could hear his heart pounding in his ears. The gun felt damp and clammy in his hand. He crouched with his back to the wall that the Tall Man would come around the corner in a moment.

A man-shape stepped around the corner. Stood there, a man-darkness, looming over him, as he raised the .45 and squeezed the trigger. And nothing happened. Another dead primer. Maybe a dead Traveler.

He stuffed the gun back under his arm, drew a knife, and lunged. He hit the man hard in the gut with his right shoulder. He figured to knock him down and cut his throat. But the guy didn't fall. It was like hitting a football tackling dummy. But this one hit back. The two men smashed and grappled at one another, turned around and around, gasping, and then—

Traveler realized that he had the wrong guy. The Tall Man was thin. This man was built like a side of beef. A lozenge-shape of blue-white chink-light lit up a corner of the stranger's face. The jock named Doug. The guy Jan had kayoed in the bar. Traveler could imagine the scenario. The guy had awakened and gone looking for them. Someone had seen Traveler duck into the alley but hadn't seen where Jan had gone. They'd told the thug, and now Traveler had two killers to contend with. . . .

The big man was forcing Traveler back, back. Pressing him against the wall.

Traveler braced, then kicked out, hit the man hard in a knee. The jock stumbled, and Traveler took advantage of the man's imbalance to trip him. The man fell to the left—

And there was a report. A *thunk*. The big man stiffened and slumped, falling at Traveler's feet.

Someone had put a bullet in him.

Traveler had glimpsed a muzzle flash from the left. The

114

Tall Man had gone out to the street and circled, coming from the direction opposite the one Traveler had expected. Had fired at Traveler, squeezed the trigger at the moment the thug had stumbled in the way.

Traveler hoped the story about the man carrying only a bullet at a time was true.

Then he heard a familiar click-snick sound of a rifle bolt. The sound of reloading.

Traveler had his back to a wall. Four feet to his right was a corner. But before he could get to it, the Tall Man—with his night-vision goggles—would shoot him down. To the left was a shallow passage, containing the oil barrel and a locked door. A dead end. Ahead, the alley continued on, but he was there. The Tall Man. He was in that deep darkness across the shallow passage, just around the corner, at the mouth of the alley's farther passage. And he was lifting the gun to his shoulder. Taking aim from about twenty feet away. Traveler ducked and knew the gun tracked down with him. At the same moment, Traveler reached into his belt, found something sharp and metallic. And Traveler could feel the crosshairs centering on his heart.

He did two things at once, then. He leapt, and as he leapt, he threw.

He snapped the ninja shuriken, razor-edged throwing star he carried in his belt, across his chest and laterally at the malevolent presence in the darkness. And he leapt across the alley.

The gun thundered, lighting up the darkness for a moment like a flashbulb.

He saw a rat in that strobe flash, scuttling to get out of his way. Then the darkness returned, and he struck the ground. Pain striped white-hot across his belly.

*I'm hit,* he thought matter-of-factly.

He was on his feet instantly and spun toward the enemy.

Suddenly, he realized that the enemy wasn't there anymore. He couldn't feel his presence. He was either gone—or dead. A lucky hit with the shuriken. The bullet had grazed Traveler, slashing across his stomach, gouging and passing on.

He fumbled in his coat and found a small metal box. He kept several rare and precious items in the box. Four matches. He decided to use one up. He had to know. He lit the match and held it up, near the alley mouth where the Tall Man had crouched. The Tall Man was sprawled there, his eyes open, staring, glazing. He lay on his side, curled up around something. A rifle lay nearby.

Traveler looked for the shuriken—and saw it. It was stuck in the wall to one side.

Then Traveler saw the crossbow shaft protruding from the killer's chest. And at the same moment he sensed someone behind him. He whirled. The match went out. Darkness. But he heard a voice.

"You were making fun when you said it. But you were right: It's a good thing I'm here to protect you." Jan's voice.

He lit another match. She was holding his crossbow.

# 13

## Drift Behind, Darkness Ahead

"They won't let us take the guns in with us," Jan said.

"Probably not," Traveler admitted. "We'll have to smuggle in what weapons we can. And steal their guns once we're inside."

"Suppose Vallone sees us?" Orwell said. He was riding up front beside Traveler this time. The Meat Wagon was in the middle of the slow-moving military caravan. There were horsemen and three guys in a jeep up ahead. More horsemen, Glory Boys, rode behind the van, guarding the truck that carried the slaves. The prisoners they'd seen in the trading depot were choking on dust in the open back of that truck and suffering from thirst in the noonday sun.

"We'll just have to hope Vallone's too busy to see us till last thing, old buddy," Traveler said. "Not sure what he'd do if he saw us. He sure wouldn't let us near any weapons, though. . . . What'd you do with your girl friend this morning?"

"Junie? She's okay. With some good people I know. Miners. An old man and his wife. She'll be okay till I get back. Damn, how come we got to go by this dirt road? My kidneys gonna be Jell-o when we get there." They jounced and wobbled over the rutted road, through a thinly dispersed forest of pine trees. The trees were too far apart to provide much shade. The sun was hot. The interior of the Meat Wagon cooked in it. The air was like molten lead. They were trying not to drink too much water. On a highway it wouldn't be so bad; at least there'd be wind in the window. Here they crawled along at no better than thirty mph.

Junie had tried to talk them out of going. It was a suicide mission, she'd said. There'd be enemies all around. Hundreds of them. They'd never come back. Saying that, she'd looked sorrowfully at Orwell.

She was probably right: It was probably a suicide mission. But as far as Traveler was concerned, postwar life was one long struggle against the perpetual probability of failure and death. And he was used to having enemies all around him.

What felt strange was having friends.

He wasn't sure if he really liked it. It felt good, being with Jan and Orwell. But it was . . . crowded. He was used to spending weeks and months alone. There was a certain lightness, a sense of freedom, that came with being alone. A freedom that almost compensated for the loneliness, and the aimlessness. Almost. Aimlessness was a companion. Loneliness was a shield. When he held Jan in his arms he felt joy, relief, warmth—and at the same time, she brought back bile-flavored memories. Memories of loss. His wife, his child, both fried to a crisp in the H-bomb explosion that took out New York City and most of New Jersey. The whole meaning in his life gone in less time than it took for a match head to burn out.

Kiel Paxton had burned up with them. Replaced by Traveler.

But Jan, just by being there, was performing a rite of necromancy. Raising the dead. Bringing Kiel Paxton back to life.

When an arm goes numb, the circulation cut off, nothing

hurts it. You can stick a needle in it and feel nothing. But when the circulation resumes, the limb comes back to life—the tingling of reawakening is painful. And after it's awake, it can be hurt again.

What's the matter, Traveler, he asked himself, you scared of a woman?

She had never told him she loved him. She showed her feelings mostly in private, with touching, with pliancy and yielding, and giving flesh for flesh. But in public, in the field, she behaved like a warrior. And yet he knew she'd chosen him. She had picked him for her mate. And that was that. She'd let him go into the maze of alleys to fight it out with the Tall Man. But she'd gotten the crossbow, had followed him back up, had shot the arrow when she'd realized that Traveler was trapped. She wasn't about to let her mate walk into a trap alone. She was serious.

And Traveler didn't think he was ready for that.

But, dammit, she was *fine*.

The convoy trundled out of the pines and set out across barren, rocky terrain, with salmon-colored boulders arching like sea monsters from the wind-waved vista of the sands. The horizon jiggled in the heat. Spit out the window and you'd hear the saliva hissing on the sands.

They were grateful for the dark when it came, bringing coolness with it. They rolled on for another hour, the horses' hooves clip-clopping through the darkness, the engines growling like desert wolves. Then Wentworth called a halt at a low hill suitable as a defensible campsite.

They found a route to the hilltop, a path wide enough for the jeep and truck and van. They arranged the vehicles in a triangle shape, the horses tied up within that perimeter. Men were posted at each angle of the triangle. Others set about cooking at a camp fire in the middle. The prisoners, cuffed to a long chain that was bolted to the truck, sat on the ground, watching the cooking, wondering if they were going to be fed. Rather grudgingly—and after the guards had been fed—Wentworth ordered the prisoners fed out of the pasty slop that passed for stew. Traveler, Jan, and Orwell ate from their own supplies, apart from the others.

Traveler and Jan were nearly asleep, lying on the cot, which he'd taken from the Meat Wagon, when a tall, one-eyed Glory Boy came to stand over him. The guy was barrel-chested, with an ape's long arms. His right eye was gone, covered with a black eye patch.

"You keep staring without an explanation, you'll lose the other eye," Traveler said.

The guy snorted. "Sure. You couldn't *reach* that eye to put it out, little fella. Listen: You got to make yourself useful. Coming along as this squaw's hired bodyguard ain't enough. Wentworth says you stand guard."

Traveler got up. He selected the Armalite and said, "Show me where."

The one-eyed Glory Boy nodded. But he was looking at Jan. His mind was elsewhere.

"Don't even think it," Traveler said. "You can pass the word. Anybody so much as breathes on her, they're dead. If I don't kill you, she will."

One-Eye snorted again. "Her?"

Jan just stared up at him, impassive.

"You ever hear of the Tall Man?" Traveler asked.

"Yeah. Saw his body this morning. Dillon had it on display. Charging a tenth-gram for a look. The Tall Man got it with an arrow. Never saw an arrow like that." Then his gaze fell on the crossbow leaning against the cot, near Jan's right arm, cocked and ready. "It was one of them—"

He looked at Traveler with new respect. "So you're the guy did the Tall Man!"

Traveler shook his head. "Nope. *She* did him in. So pass the word."

One-Eye looked at Jan. She smiled distantly.

120

He took a nervous step back from her. "Uh, sure. Your post is this way."

He led Traveler to a six-foot gap between the long truck and the jeep. Traveler leaned against the rear of the jeep, wishing he had a cigarette. Tobacco was a rare thing to find.

Two hours passed. The darkness outside the firelight was nearly complete. A little starlight silvered boulder rims and bushes. The plain was a sea of shadow.

But as he watched, a point of light winked on in the sea of darkness. It grew and danced. A camp fire. Only one. Probably salvagers or miners. No one to worry about.

Nightbirds hooed, and some insect called redundantly for its mate.

Then he heard the guards talking behind him. "Figure it's a big camp?"

"Naw. But you never know. The army can always use one or two more."

"Shit, I was just getting to sleep. . . ."

Twenty minutes later, One-Eye led half a dozen men out into the night. Armed and ready.

Just before they'd left, Traveler had heard Wentworth say, "If there are too many of them, you sustain too many losses, give it up."

"How many is too many losses, sir?" One-Eye had asked.

"Three. No, make it four. . . ."

Orwell came and tapped Traveler on the shoulder. He said, around a yawn, "They sent me to relieve you."

Traveler nodded. He glanced at the cot. Jan was asleep. "I've got to check something out, man. I'll be back before long."

Orwell started to object, but Traveler had already melted into the night.

# 14

## Shadows Take a Vengeance

"You're a fool," Traveler told himself. "You're a jerk. A sucker. A sentimental mush-brain."

Right now he could be back at the camp, lying beside Jan, sleeping. He could have used the sleep. Out here he might run into anything. Bloats, wild-dog pack, roadrats, rattlers.

But he'd come out here, anyway. He knew the camp fire was probably some harmless survivors just trying to make it through another day. He knew, also, that Wentworth had sent out a party to capture them. To enslave them. It was none of his business. He couldn't save the fucking world.

He shrugged as he moved through the night, loping between the boulders, down the hillside. What the hell.

This gave him the chance to frustrate the Glory Boys. They'd pissed him off. In a way, this was going to be a pleasure.

If he didn't get killed doing it.

He reached the flatter ground and stopped to listen. He could hear the crunch of footsteps up ahead. The Glory Boys, moving toward the camp fire.

Traveler had to get there first.

It was dark, but away from the firelight his eyes had

122

adjusted. He could make out rocks and stunted trees and fissures in the ground. The desert had gone silent as the night animals sensed the intruders. It seemed dead.

Traveler sprinted where the ground was clear, picked his way hurriedly when there were obstacles. He passed the Glory Boys, keeping the bigger boulders between them and him. He heard them whisper complaints now and then. One-Eye told them to shut up.

Traveler's heart was thudding, his breathing ragged. Spent too much time riding in the Meat Wagon. Not in shape for running. Have to do something about that. But mornings out in your jogging togs wasn't in anymore.

He ran and tripped, fell headlong into the dirt. He almost swore but bit it off, wary of alerting the Glory Boys.

He got to his hands and knees, felt for the rifle, found it—and froze.

A sound had made him freeze. A familiar sound, like someone shaking maracas warningly fast, close by. Rattlesnake.

He could sense it now. It was a presence that felt as cold as a living machine. It radiated imminent violence. And it was a big one.

Maybe if he didn't move it wouldn't strike. It would relax or slither away. He was on his knees, gun butt in his hands, motionless.

But he could feel it drawing its head back to strike.

It was about two feet from his right elbow, just beneath a rock overhang. Coiled up on another rock. He could see it only faintly.

But he could feel its life force emanating from a tiny node in its head; that node, in Traveler's mind's eye, was like a glowing red jewel, hard and cold and bright as a ruby, and like a ruby, the color of blood.

The rattler struck.

Traveler struck at the same moment, letting his reflexes do the aiming, his *ki* force concentrating in his hands, transferring to the gun held across his body. He struck sideways, hard as a jeweler striking a chisel into a big ruby. A mad jeweler who wanted to smash the ruby.

The gun butt caught the rattler in the teeth, smashed its head back, dashing its pea-sized brain out against the overhanging rock.

Traveler felt its life force snuff out. He wiped the rifle butt on the sand and got to his feet. He heard a man's voice hissing: "Sure, I'm sure, man. I heard a noise over here. Kind of noise a man makes. Hitting something."

Bootsteps behind him. He could sense them thirty feet away.

He got down and rolled into the protection of the overhanging rock. He was lying atop the cold body of the snake, feeling its blood soak through his sleeve.

Carefully, he laid the rifle aside, picked up the snake, and threw it at the legs of the man coming parallel to him.

The man shouted. There was a spurt of gunfire. "Fucking rattler jumped at me! Shit!"

Two other men, just silhouettes in the darkness, ran up from behind. "You dumb fuck! The target's gonna know we're here!" One-Eye's voice.

"The snake nearly killed me, man, what am I supposed to do?"

"All right, all right, keep your voice down. Looks like you got the snake. Good for you. Put it in your pack, we'll have it for breakfast. Good eating . . . Okay, come on. We lost surprise, but we probably got 'em outnumbered."

Traveler lay stone-still as they passed. He counted to forty, then got up, and once more ran to circle them, getting ahead of them.

He saw the camp fire up ahead. A bubble of glow in the darkness. There were two men and a woman standing by

124

the fire. The woman had a year-old infant in her arms. One of the men was at least sixty, the other was a young man. Both carried rifles. All three looked out into the darkness. They looked scared. A buckboard with a tired-looking, bony horse was tied up behind them. Even the horse had its ears twitched up, its eyes rolling nervously. They'd heard the gunshots.

The old man spoke to his companions. The three moved back into the darkness outside the firelight, taking cover in the rocks.

Traveler smiled. It was working out, so far.

He ran in a crouch around the ring of firelight, careful to stay in the shadow. He could hear the Glory Boys approaching. They weren't exactly light-footed.

He came around behind the buckboard. He looked over his shoulder, saw the old man ushering the young one and the woman, with her child, up into a tumble of boulders that looked like a miniature Transylvanian castle. They were about a hundred and fifty feet behind Traveler. Traveler's guess was that they'd hold their fire till their hiding place was discovered. But that heap of rock was the first place the Glory Boys would look.

So it would be best if the Glory Boys thought that the owners of the buckboard were right here. He checked the clip on the Armalite.

The AR-180 was a light assault rifle firing standard U.S. military 5.56 rounds. It wasn't as accurate as the HK91, but it was lighter. He'd wanted something easy to run with. And it was effective up to about a hundred seventy-five yards. The enemy was only about thirty yards away. And closing.

He closed his eyes and, mentally, reached out to sense their whereabouts. The seven men were spread out in a line with about twenty feet between each, moving steadily in toward the camp fire. Then he saw a big bald-headed guy faintly outlined by the outer reaches of the firelight. The guy was raising his head over a boulder, looking around, trying to figure out where the inhabitants of the campsite had gone.

He opened his mouth and said something to someone unseen near him. Traveler couldn't hear it, but he could imagine it. *You think they're behind that buckboard—or maybe run off into the desert?*

Traveler gave him what he hoped they'd take as an answer.

He laid the Armalite across the wood of the buckboard, steadied it, aimed at the bald head, and pulled the trigger. The bald head exploded like an egg shot with a pellet gun. The horse snorted and moved uneasily in its harness. But it didn't spook. It looked over its shoulder at him quizzically.

"It's okay, fella," he said, trying to emanate reassurance. It quieted down. Maybe it was used to gunfire.

Anyway, it held its ground when the buckboard began to spit splinters as slugs bit into it. Return fire from the Glory Boys. They couldn't see him, but they'd seen the muzzle flash and knew about where he was. Thinking he was the buckboard's owner defending the campsite.

He squeezed off a three-round burst at one of their muzzle flashes and ducked behind the buckboard. Bullets sang into it, chewing it up badly. The horse would get it sooner or later.

Traveler crept to the horse, untied it, and led it by its halter into the darkness.

He heard someone shout, "They're making a break for it!"

Traveler smiled and slapped the horse's rump, hard.

The old nag leapt ahead, clattering into the desert, the buckboard rattling along behind it. Traveler threw himself down behind a low boulder.

The Glory Boys, as Traveler had hoped, poured their

fire into the buckboard, assuming their targets were there. Then the shooting stopped as One-Eye reminded his men they were there to capture, not to kill.

One-Eye shouted, "Surrender or we'll cut you down! If you're wounded we'll give you medical treatment!"

Traveler snorted, thinking, lying mother-rapers.

He was skirting the collapsing bubbling of light around the dying camp fire now, circling behind the Glory Boys. But he had no definite fix on their positions—they were lined up relative to him, now, and that confused his proximity sense.

So he nearly ran into one of them head-on. A pop-eyed guy with an undershot jaw and bulging biceps. He gaped at Traveler and blurted, "Hey you're that guy who—"

Traveler shut him up with a mouthful of lead.

He pumped a burst of three slugs into the guy at a range of four feet, blowing his teeth out through the back of his head.

The Glory Boy fell ingloriously back, arms akimbo. Traveler had to repress the urge to strip him of ammo and weapons. No time. The others were making a lot of noise as they jogged toward the sound of gunfire.

Three of them together. Too dark, too much in the way to be sure of getting them all. They were wary, too. And he'd have to get them or he could be pinned down here. Time to back off.

"Jesus!" one of the Glory Boys yelled as Traveler slipped back into the sagebrush. "They got Frog! Shit, this was supposed to be easy! Benny said he saw an old man a girl and one guy. They some pretty good shots, man!"

One-Eye's voice: "Keep your head and your voice down, dumb ass. Brick, you take the point. We go after that buckboard. The horse stopped runnin'—I can see it. See it over there, against that hill?"

Traveler started moving, fast.

He was moving in the deepest areas of darkness. But his hyperacute senses kept him from stumbling. The fall that had almost thrown him into a rattler had waked him up. Having a rattler strike at you works better than caffeine.

He got to the buckboard before they did. The horse was serenely pulling up clumps of some plant with its teeth.

Traveler reached out, sensing the whereabouts of the oncoming Glory Boys.

They were about thirty yards to the left, down the slope a little. He moved off to their flank, ducked behind a boulder, and waited.

They were coming on in a loose V, about ten feet between them, a big guy in a red leather suit taking the point.

He waited till red-suit was twenty feet past him, heading toward the buckboard.

He got to his knees. He left one knee on the ground, the other he crooked, boot on the dirt, to use as a prop for the rifle. He centered his sights, just a faint dot in the starlight, on the red-leather back of the man who'd passed him.

"Hey, there's somebody behind that rock with a gun pointed at your back, Luke!" someone shouted from Traveler's left.

Traveler squeezed the trigger. The Armalite roared, spat fire, kicking at his shoulder. Luke screamed and spun, his spine shot through.

Traveler snapped the gun around toward the voice that had called out the warning. He had to get that one. If the guy had seen him, he could go back to camp and tell them just who he'd seen. . . .

The man was running, his back to Traveler. Traveler sprayed hard, using up most of his clip, zigzagging the rounds across his target. The man grunted and fell.

That's four, he thought.

One-Eye shouted, "That's four! There must be a lot more of 'em we didn't spot! Pull back! Regroup!"

Traveler lingered awhile to make sure. The Glory Boys were heading back to their camp.

Traveler tied the horse to a bush. He hoped the owners would find it and use it to get the hell out of there.

He took a deep breath and started off toward the hilltop camp where the Glory Boys just might be waiting for him. If someone had noticed he was gone, they'd put two and two together.

He pushed himself hard, till sweat ran in rivulets down his back, to get ahead of the Glory Boys and up the hill.

He had to come the last thirty feet silently as possible, so as not to attract the attention of the guards. He made it and snuck up to Orwell. Orwell grinned, seeing him coming. "Tell you about it tomorrow," Traveler said.

He slipped unnoticed into camp, went to his cot—and found it empty. Jan was gone.

# 15

## The Valley of Fire

One-Eye was telling Wentworth, "Would I bullshit you, sir? There was at least twenty of 'em! I mean, for chrissakes, they got four of our boys! You want to see the bodies, we can take a walk. Sir."

Traveler was trying to decide what to do. She wasn't in the van, or in the camp. He knew what had happened. She'd waked up, found him gone, and had gone looking for him, to cover his back. Maybe she'd heard the men talking about the slavers who'd been sent out, had realized what Traveler was up to. She'd be back soon, realizing she'd missed the action. And then—

She came strolling nonchalantly into camp, the HK assault rifle under her arm.

Wentworth's eyes narrowed.

"Hey," somebody said. "She was out there. She don't like us none. Maybe she was helping those slave-meats. . . ."

Wentworth considered it. He and Jan looked at one another. She did a pretty good job of looking confused. "What's the big deal? I got to get permission to take a piss?" she asked.

"Yeah," Wentworth said. "You do."

"Maybe she wasn't pissing," said the skeptic, a guy with half his face covered in burn scars. "Maybe she—"

He broke off when Wentworth waved his hand dismissively. "She's just a woman. She was taking a piss, that's all."

For a moment One-Eye looked as if he might say something. He knew who had killed the Tall Man. He knew she wasn't "just a woman." But Traveler could guess One-Eye's reasoning. No matter how good a fighter the girl was, it would look bad if One-Eye had let a single woman outmatch him and his men. He played along. "Ah, let her pee when she wants to."

Wentworth returned to his discussion with One-Eye.

Jan returned to the cot and laid the gun aside. She and Traveler lay down, side by side. Then the whispering began.

"Traveler, dammit, why didn't you tell me you were going? I hunted all over for you! I thought you'd—"

"Never mind. You've got to let me do a few things on my own. I'm a big boy now."

He could feel her stiffen. She didn't like that.

He was too tired to care. Sleep came and took him for a long ride.


The next morning, he woke up, stood, streched, looked around—and felt awe. It looked as if the world were on fire.

They were in a valley whose enclosing walls were made of fiery red sandstone. The sandstone was uniformly red, all the way around. The valley's upper slopes and walls were wind-carved into abstracts, into gargoylish columns and clinkers that looked like frozen crimson smoke. He seemed to make out tormented semihuman shapes writhing in the configuration of the high banks of stone, like souls burning in hell. The morning sunlight exaggerated the redness of the rock, and the heat-shimmer made it seem to shimmy like flames.

131

It was like a monument to the Third World War.

"The Valley of Fire," Jan said, bringing him coffee and hot biscuits. "A sacred place. Many old Indian pictoglyphs."

Half an hour later they were trundling through the valley, following a sand-blurred road. There wasn't much vegetation here. They could see a long way to either side and felt relatively safe from ambush. Sounds seemed to have a life of their own in the Valley of Fire, each clop of horses' hooves or creak of the van seeming unnaturally pronounced. A red plume of dust rose behind the caravan.

Now and then One-Eye would ride by the van on his horse, trotting up to speak to the men up front and check out the route. As he passed he'd turn his single red eye on Traveler and Jan. He'd been thinking. Probably he suspected both them of having been involved in last night's action. He could be a problem later.

The day scraped by, slow and grinding as a mechanical snail. The dust choked them. They were running low on water and had to restrict themselves to one swallow apiece, once an hour, though the heat made them yearn to be drinking water constantly. The reflective sand of the valley, the shadowless flatness around them—the rocks were a quarter of a mile off—made the place into an enormous sun-reflection oven.

The caravan procession began to elongate as the tired horses fell behind. The prisoners groaned and swore and whimpered in their dusty, baking truckbed. Traveler drove grimly on, thinking about El Hiagura and Vallone. . . .

No one ever said that a satisfying vengeance would come easy.

When the soldiers ahead and behind were out of earshot, Orwell asked, "You gonna tell me, man?" He was sitting in the back, on the cot, leaning against a bullet-proof vest, looking over Traveler's shoulder out the dusty windshield.

"Tell you what? Why my van isn't air-conditioned?"

"Now that you mention it. But I was thinking about last night."

"Wanted to cut down the odds a little. The Glory Assholes went out to capture some more slaves. I went out and pretended to be the targets shooting back at the Glories. Cut down the odds by four."

"Bullshit," Jan said. "He's soft-hearted. Wanted to save some salvager family from slavery. Risked our whole mission doing it."

"That's closer to what I figured," Orwell said, chuckling.

Traveler glanced at her, wondering if she were really pissed off at him. She looked out the windshield, expressionless. He reached out and put his hand over hers. She took his hand—and bit it.

"Shit!" Traveler blurted, snatching his hand back.

Jan and Orwell laughed. She leaned over and kissed him. "Sorry," she said. "I couldn't resist."

"*Learn* to resist," Traveler said.

But he felt better because she was smiling now.

"Maybe what we ought to do," Orwell began, "is—"

They never found out what he was going to suggest. He broke off, frowning. "What's that noise?"

Traveler shook his head. "I don't hear—oh. You mean that buzzing noise? Like, up and down?"

"Yeah."

It was a drone that came in waves, and at the peak of the wave, it was powerfully loud. It was like the sound of a buzz saw being turned on and off. Just as the buzz saw was slowing down, near stopping, it would be turned on again.

"Oh, shit," Jan said.

"What is it?" Traveler asked, looking at her. There was a look of recognition on her face.

She said an Indian name he could never pronounce. "It means Fire's Teeth," she said. "I didn't say anything about it because I thought they came later in the season. And I never thought they'd attack so many people.''

"They? What are *they*? And how do you know they're attacking?"

"That's their attack call. Pull up to the jeep, I've got to talk to Wentworth."

"What the fuck is a Fire's Teeth?" Orwell was asking.

Traveler accelerated, coming up behind the jeep on the left so Jan could open the shutters, lean out, and shout at Wentworth in the back of the jeep. "We've got to get to full-speed!" she shouted. "The horsemen got to go to gallop!"

"What the hell are you talking about?" Wentworth shouted back. "I can't hear most of it!"

The buzz-wave of warning was getting louder, more grating.

"Plug your ears and run for it," Jan shouted. "Fire's Teeth! Don't you know? Haven't you come through here before?"

"This is a new route—the other one was blown up," Wentworth shouted. "Pull over and tell me what the fuck—"

He broke off, clapping his hands to his ears, shouting with pain.

Traveler was gritting his teeth with pain too: The buzzing drone had hit some frequency painful to his ears. He felt like crawling into the sand and burying his head. And realized that whatever the Fire's Teeth was, it must want him to do just that.

Orwell shouted unintelligibly as the buzz became a painful shriek vibrating through the metal of the van. It made the dust form itself into sound-wave shapes on the windshield. A glass cover cracked on one of the dashboard dials.

Orwell lit a candle in the back, which seemed a strange

134

thing to do, till Traveler saw him dripping wax on a wad of fibers he'd taken from the lining of a sleeping bag. He passed Traveler the cooling lump, and they plugged their ears with it. Jan was still shouting out the window. She accepted an earplug. It helped. The pain became mild irritation. But they could hear men screaming, horses neighing; the truck behind them was out of control. Jan pointed out the window, across Traveler.

From the left: a wave of living redness.

It was as if the valley walls had begun to crumple and crawl toward them. But as the wave of red came closer, like surf running up a sunset-crimsoned beach, Traveler could make out its components. Kangaroo rats? Scarabs?

Mutants. Insects on long hind legs, hopping toward them. Each one with five-inch legs, a four-inch body. Four smaller, clawed legs under the hard red carapace. Face like a spider with sharp, serrated mandibles. Bounding toward them on those hind legs. Thousands. Maybe millions of them. A wave, a horde of them, coming on like locusts or army ants. But so many more than army ants, and so much more vicious than locusts, and so much bigger than either. Jackrabbits and snakes ran and slithered ahead of the horde. Were overtaken. Were covered over. Were reduced to nothing in seconds.

Traveler could feel the horde's single-minded purpose as it approached. It radiated a message on the psychic wavelengths. The message was simple:

*Kill and eat. Kill and eat. Kill and eat. Kill . . .*

Traveler hit the gas, and the Meat Wagon lurched ahead.

The insects closed in from the left, swarming over the road. Horses shrieked and bolted. Some of them bolted the wrong way and ran into the mass of hungry desert mutations. Shiny-backed, rat-sized insects leaped up onto the horse's flanks, clung with their little forearms, and began to gnaw.

The horse reared and whinnied, throwing the rider, who fell screaming into the moiling sea of insects. In seconds he was covered over. He got to his feet, covered head to foot in clinging, gnawing insects, a man made out of insects, and staggered, screaming, until they clawed their way down his throat and clogged it so he couldn't scream anymore and then he fell and . . .

Traveler left the scene behind, cutting in the four-wheel drive to grind on over the Fire's Teeth horde boiling over the road, feeling them squash under the wheels, wondering if they could gnaw through tires. . . .

He heard panicky Glory Boys stupidly wasting their ammo, firing into the mass.

Jan shouted, ''Close your windows!''

Traveler reached over to pull the metal shutter closed. Another wave of the swarm seemed to wash up against the truck then, and three Fire's Teeth leapt through the window. One fell on the floor, one landed on the steering column, another on Traveler's thigh. The Fire's Teeth immediately took firm grip on his trousers and began chewing. . . .

He slammed the shutter, then slapped at the insect beginning to gnaw at the skin of his leg. It held on, lifting its head to snap at his hand. ''You little shit!'' he shouted. He tore it off his leg, skin crawling at the touch of the verminous thing, feeling its hairy underbelly bristling on his palm. It dug its claws into his palm and took a bite out of the soft part of his hand between thumb and forefinger. ''Damn!'' He smashed it again and again on the steering wheel, all the time trying to steer around panicky horses and the thicker areas of the swarm.

Finally the thing let go, fell dead to the floor. But another was gnawing on his ankles.

Jan reached down and cut it loose with a knife. Then she used the blade to kill the other two.

Traveler's hand was swelling. He felt nauseated. The

136

hand was going numb. "It's poisonous," he said. He felt a chill as she nodded.

"But the poison's not lethal unless you get at least ten bites. Which you could easily get out there. You might get paralysis in that hand for a few hours. . . ." She took his hand in hers and sucked the poison out, spat it on the floor. She applied an herb-paste dressing from a leather bag she carried on her belt.

Meanwhile, steering with his left hand, Traveler had reached the front of the column. But the swarm was still all around the Meat Wagon, and now it was in layers, insects atop insects, so the swarm was two feet thick here. The van was beginning to skid on the smashed bodies, the insect slime oozing under the wheels. It was losing traction. He put it in high gear and jerked the wheel from side to side, weaving. If they lost traction they could get stuck. The little fuckers would work their way into the van somehow. . . .

Then he broke out of the swarm and was in the open desert again. It looked clean, beautifully clean.

He looked in the rearview mirror, was relieved to see the prisoners' truck coming through. And was disappointed to see that Wentworth's jeep had made it. Also about half the horsemen, including One-Eye, came galloping out of the swarm. Men in the truck and the jeep were throwing insects out, smashing them, plucking them off arms and legs. The horsemen used quirts to slap them from their mounts. The horses were streaked in blood, staggering from the poison.

By mutual tacit consent, no one stopped to reassess the status of the column just then. They drove or rode as fast as they could, to get the hell out of there. Traveler drove with his left hand; Jan shifted for him. She'd gotten most of the poison out. After an hour, his hand felt sore but usable.

Two hours later, Wentworth signaled a halt. They'd left the Valley of Fire behind and were now in the open, flat, yellowish wasteland scarred with ravines and bristly with desert shrubs. Wentworth had stopped in the shade of a heap of boulders that threw long easterly shadows in the late afternoon light.

They assessed the damage. Only three of the prisoners had died. They'd cooperated to keep the bugs off one another. But one of them had been overwhelmed. Most of his face was gnawed away. The skull showed through, and the eyes were gone. Wentworth checked the corpse's pockets, found nothing valuable, and had it unchained and tossed into a ravine.

Traveler heard a Glory Boy shakily telling, "I was in the jeep and I turned around to shout something to Arnie, and he was all covered by bugs. Must have been fifty of them leapt on him all at once. I started knocking them off and the ones who were on his head—it was like they realized I wasn't going to let them eat in peace. So they . . . they'd been gnawing on his neck . . . and they removed his head, all working together to do it, and jumped off the jeep with it. . . ."

One of the horses was hobbling mostly on three legs. The fourth leg was chewed through to the bone in spots. It had to be shot.

About half the men there—and most of the prisoners— were sick from the poison. When the guards weren't looking, Jan used her herbs to administer to as many of the prisoners as she could.

Traveler helped her. He rubbed salve on an old man's arm wound. It was the same old man he'd heard swearing at the guards in the trading depot. The gutsy one who'd told them just what he thought. He had three days' growth of white beard and tufted white eyebrows, blue eyes clear as mountain icewater. He was a florid old man, and dour.

138

"You got a Marine Corps tattoo, I see," Traveler said.

"That's right. You look like you was military once, boy."

"I was. Army. Saw a little action in El Hiagura. Listen, you remember how to fire an M16?"

The old man snorted. "Just put one in my hands."

"I just might do that. Later. What's your name?"

"Thorne. Bob Thorne."

"I'm Traveler. Listen, uh"—he lowered his voice to a whisper—"if you know a few people you figure could keep their mouths shut," Traveler went on, "tell them they're going to get a chance to go free. Those who want to go. They should be ready to risk their asses. To grab any guns they can get their hands on. And to keep real quiet about it till then."

The old man shook his hand. "I'll see to it. Just put the thing in my hand. . . ." He smiled grimly.

Wentworth shouted, "Okay, let's move out. Another hour and we're there."

# 16

## The Killing Ground

"I oughta be happy to get that fucking trip over with," Orwell was saying as they rumbled through the gates of the army outpost, "but what I feel is real nervous. Like I was going into the penitentiary."

It looked like a prison camp from the outside. Like a World War Two German camp for POWs. Fifteen-foot metal-mesh fences topped with Y-post barbed wire. A wooden machine-gun tower. A dusty compound, and a U-shaped arrangement of Quonset huts, plus a large, ominous-looking gray concrete building with barred windows: Slave quarters.

They pulled up behind the jeep and in front of the wooden administration building. It was painted green and recently built.

Traveler got out, looking for weak points.

The gate was doubly reinforced steel wire. Power for the base was transmitted through buried cables from Base Zero, five miles off. Jan had told him that. She'd been investigating the base for a long time.

One of the Quonset huts was nearly twice as big as the others. There was a guard at the front entrance. Probably the storage dump for NT77.

They hadn't managed to contact Danny. Wentworth had

140

insisted they come to the base under guard. An hour earlier, they'd seen the raiding party, Danny riding out front, riding parallel to their course on the hilltops, a quarter of a mile off, classic Indian-Recon style. But the chance to break away from Wentworth and meet with Danny and set up the timing hadn't come. They'd just have to hope that Danny was observing them. That he'd realize—

Traveler's train of thought was derailed when Wentworth, One-Eye, and two other men, SMGs in their hands pointing at Traveler, walked up, faces stony. Jan had come around the van to stand beside Traveler. Orwell stood on the other side.

"You'll have to give up the guns," Wentworth said. "Now."

Traveler hesitated.

The guards cocked their submachine guns. They'd gun him down before he got his weapon into firing position.

Traveler shrugged, as though it didn't matter. "We just carry 'em out of habit. You're here to protect us from roadrats, we don't need 'em. But when we leave . . ."

Wentworth smiled. Traveler didn't like that smile. "You'll get them back," Wentworth said.

Traveler passed his rifle over. Jan did the same. "I'll stay with the van," Orwell said. That was part of a tentative plan they'd worked out. He added, "I'll need this gun to protect the van."

"The guards will protect it," Wentworth said.

"Who'll protect it from the guards?" Traveler asked. "Everything on this machine is valuable. The engine parts, the weapons, the supplies in it—"

"It'll be impounded till you're ready to leave. I'll be personally responsible for its protection," Wentworth said wearily. He was dusty and tired.

Reluctantly, Orwell gave up the Thompson; One-Eye

carried the weapons off in his arms like a bundle of firewood. He stowed them in the admin building and returned, grinning.

Wentworth held out his hand. "The keys to the van," he said.

Controlling his impulse to say "Over my dead body," Traveler tossed Wentworth the keys. Wentworth gave them to One-Eye.

"This way," Wentworth said. He turned away. Traveler, Jan, and Orwell followed him. The guards came along behind, guns at ready. Traveler felt uncomfortably like a prisoner being escorted to jail.

Behind them, One-Eye started the van and drove it to a metal shed where other vehicles were locked up.

The sun was melting over the hilly horizon, suffusing the air with reddish light which made the stark buildings and the dusty spaces between seem unreal, abstract shapes in some painter's "red period."

They walked across to the detention center, presumably to see Jan's brother, as proof he was still alive. They went in through rusty metal doors that had been cannibalized from some ruined building elsewhere, past a guard at a wooden desk who snapped to attention as Wentworth came in, and down a long hallway to another metal door. This one Wentworth unlocked, using keys from a weighty ring attached to his belt by an extendable wire. They went through the door, and Wentworth locked it behind them. They entered a concrete stairway smelling of fresh paint, stark white in the light from a naked overhead bulb, and climbed, footsteps echoing, to the second floor.

The detention hall was a long gallery extending the length of the rectangular building with a series of steel-barred cells on the right, accessed by a narrow corridor. The air was close. There were barred windows at either end of the corridor but none in the cells. Instead of toilets,

142

each cell had a sort of trough. There were no sinks or water sources. No bunks. Prisoners slept on the floor, one small blanket apiece. Each cell was made to hold twenty prisoners. There were at least forty to a cell. Those who'd been brought in with Wentworth's transport were already here.

There was a small anteroom-office at the head of the stairs, just before the metal door leading into the cell-block corridor. Wentworth paused here and said, "Before you see the boy, I have to be sure you aren't carrying any other weapons. Can't take a chance you might slip one to the prisoners."

One of the guards—the one with half his face burned, whom Traveler thought of as Scarface—frisked them. He was particularly thorough with Jan. Traveler controlled his temper, seeing the guard's hands linger on Jan's curves. Scarface found nothing but tactile titillation on Jan; on Traveler he found a knife. He confiscated that, passing it to Wentworth with a lopsided grin. Pleased with himself.

But Scarface had missed the Shuriken stars, hidden in a slit in Traveler's belt.

Wentworth motioned to a guard who stood by the metal door. The guard unlocked it and held it for them as they walked through. The stench would have choked a maggot.

Sallow angry, despairing empty hollow-eyed faces looked out from between the bars. Concentration-camp faces. They stopped at the third cell. There were four in all.

"Martin Luther King Plainwalker, front and center," Wentworth shouted.

The crowd of the miserable parted. An Indian boy, maybe seventeen years old, came to the bars, and as everyone in such circumstances seems to do instinctively, he closed his fists around two of them.

"Martin . . ." Jan said. Her voice broke, but she controlled it and said, "We've come to bargain you out of there. We're going to give them something they want in exchange for letting you go.''

She was saying this for Wentworth's benefit, but Martin didn't know that.

"Don't give these animals anything useful," he said. "I don't want to get out knowing my freedom gave them more power."

"We'll give them what we have to," she said.

"No!"

But she'd turned away. "Let's go see Vallone," she said impassively.

Wentworth nodded and led them up the corridor.

The two guards with the SMGs were behind them. They'd gotten used to him and had lowered their guns. It would only take them a second to raise them and fire, but they might hesitate with Wentworth up ahead. Wentworth could easily be hit too. Maybe now was the time . . . the time to spin around, kick out, knock one guard into another, grab a weapon. . .

But no: There was a guard outside the door into the corridor. And Wentworth was armed. It might not be so easy to take him hostage. The anteroom would be a better place. . . .

"Hey, officer," said someone from the cell beside the door. "There's another dead one in here."

Wentworth paused to look through the bars. Traveler followed his gaze.

Two prisoners were carrying a body, holding it up by the armpits. They laid it out on the concrete floor, beside the bars. The body of a fourteen-year-old girl. Blue-white. Emaciated. A mat of blood covering one side of her scalp.

"The claustrophobia got to her," said the man who'd spoken first. "She wouldn't eat for a couple days, then she up and smashed her head on the—"

"Spare me the tear-jerking details," Wentworth said

144

dryly. "I'll have her taken out when I have time." He added, to himself, "I suppose the labs could use her for dissection."

Traveler thought, Your time is coming, asshole.

Wentworth unlocked the door and they went out into the anteroom.

Someone had arrived in the anteroom while they were in the cell block. Vallone.

"Hello, Paxton," he said.

He was pointing a .44 Magnum at Traveler's chest.

# 17

## And the Killing

"I got a message from an old friend of yours a few minutes ago," Vallone was saying. "The Black Rider. He sent someone to tell me that a man who calls himself Traveler, once known as Kiel Paxton, was coming here looking for me. He said he didn't know why you were looking for me." He spoke archly, smiling, as if telling an anecdote. "He said something about getting garbled mental transmissions from you. But he was sure you were looking for me with something like vengeance in mind. . . ."

Traveler shrugged. There was no use denying it. Vallone would never take a chance on him. He'd kill him, just to be sure.

"Well, hello, Orwell," Vallone said, nodding politely at the black man.

"You got it all wrong, Vallone," Orwell said. "We come here on a job. Bodyguarding this lady. Thass all."

Vallone laughed. "Of course you did. And I came here because I thought it was a good spot for a vacation." He let the sarcasm hang in the air for a moment before continuing, "You fellows will be seeing your old friend The Black Rider in a couple of days. He wants you alive—in chains. So he can deal with you his way. I'm going to trade you to him in return for a few favors. He reads minds, it seems.

He could be useful to me. So I'm going to have to ask you to step back into that cell block."

"What about my brother?" Jan demanded.

"That deal is still on. But it does not include the lives of these two gentlemen. We'll lock them up, and you'll come with me."

They were locked in the least crowded cell, with Martin. Old Thorne was there too. Jan had gone with Vallone, without a backward glance.

Orwell, Martin, Thorne, and Traveler stood together by the bars. The corridor was empty. The prisoners had been silent, out of fear, when Wentworth had come in. Now a droning lamentation started up. Women and children sobbing. Men muttering. Orwell turned to Traveler and asked, "Now what?"

Traveler said, "I've still got the shuriken. Jan and Danny are on the outside. We'll look for our chance. Or we won't get one, and we'll die."

"What are you talking about?" Martin asked, looking back and forth between them.

"We aren't here to bargain," Traveler said. "We came to break you out. . . ."

Martin shook his head and smiled sadly. "Jan is crazy. She was never afraid of anything. She's going to get herself killed for nothing." He looked thoughtful. "There's someone here you should talk to. He was a guard. He was . . . different from the others. He argued with Wentworth about the way we were treated, and Wentworth threw him in here. He knows how this place is put together. He might be able to help. Hey, Carter!"

A short, thick man with blue rings of weariness under his eyes introduced himself as Carter. He wore fatigues, army boots, and a grimy T-shirt. Sweat beaded his forehead.

It was hot and sticky in the cell. The crying, whim-

147

pering, and cursing came and went in swells; some of the prisoners were abject, silent, hunched up in their own little spaces against the walls, staring into a nightmare future.

Traveler shook Carter's hand with a genuine warmth. Carter must have known he'd be in deep shit for arguing with Wentworth.

"No one's tried a jailbreak yet?" Traveler asked.

"They tried to riot once," Carter said, shaking his head. "Wentworth got the guys who started it and had them tortured where everyone could see. Then he sent them to the labs. Downstairs. He left the lab windows open so we could hear. Heard 'em scream when they tested things on them. That's when I spoke up. He threw me in here. I'm supposed to go to the labs tomorrow." There was no self-pity in his voice. "Another time somebody tried to grab one of the guards. But they always came in twos. They got the one guy, but the guards are under orders not to 'accept a hostage situation.' So the other one did what we were told to do: He shot the guy who'd grabbed the guard, and the guard too. Things weren't so bad when General Harker was in charge. But Vallone got him arrested. And executed."

"Yes, sir, there's a lot of benefits to a career in the army," Orwell said.

"You know how to get to the ordnance, Carter?" Traveler asked.

"There's a rack of guns in the office out there. Locked up. And there's a little of everything in the basement. . . . I know where it's being stored down there, and how to get to it."

Traveler nodded. "Okay. When do the guards feed you?"

"Twice a day. Revolting crap for breakfast, one bowl each. For dinner we have something else: disgusting slop, instead. That'll be anytime now. Maybe ten minutes or

148

so. They bring it here on a cart, pass bowls through that slot there . . .''

"All right. When they come in, you guys push the crowd back so I've got room to move. Before then, ask around, see who's got experience with automatic weapons or any other kind of military weapon. Bring them up front."

"Okay."

Traveler turned to watch the door at the other end of the corridor.

In ten minutes they'd found four willing men who'd had experience with automatic weapons. Three of them were past fifty but looked steady. The fourth was a grim-eyed black youth who never spoke, except to identify himself as Slam Sam.

The others asked a lot of nervous questions. They seemed doubtful of their chances for success. But they also didn't seem to care. They'd had enough. They were ready to die fighting.

And then the door opened. A guard came in, held the door for the other one, who pushed a cart through. On the cart was an enormous metal pot. He left the cart in the corridor and went out for another like it. Then they locked the door and came in. They pushed the carts down toward the end of the hall; the routine was to start at the end cell and work back toward the door.

They came abreast of Traveler's cell, on their way to the one at the end. Scarface looked annoyed. Apparently he'd drawn guard duty after a long day on the trail. Evidently he didn't consider that fair.

He glanced at Traveler in passing and grinned, pleased with Traveler's predicament. He'd envied that shiny black van.

The grin faded from his face when Traveler lifted the

149

shuriken-throwing star over his head, snapped his arm down, and threw.

Scarface opened his mouth to shout a warning, but all that came out was, "Uck!" as one of the points on the four-pointed star sank, *chunk,* into his skull, between his eyes.

Before he'd hit the ground, Traveler had flung the other star. The other guard was turning, gaping, lifting the SMG. And the second star missed its mark. It sank into his right eye, instead. But the man screamed, overwhelmed by pain, and dropped the gun. It clattered within Orwell's reach. He reached through the bars and grabbed it. Traveler was dragging Scarface's body near, by the ankle. He jerked the keys from Scarface's belt.

The other guard had plucked the throwing star from his bloody eye socket, was running toward the door.

"Shoot him!" Thorne urged Orwell.

"No!" Traveler said, unlocking the cell door. "That'll alert the guy out in the office. Somebody grab him!"

The corridor was narrow. Someone stuck a leg through the bars, down the hall, and tripped the wounded guard. He went sprawling. Traveler stepped out, retrieved his shuriken, and ran to the fallen guard.

The man rolled over onto his back, was reaching for a club on his belt and opening his mouth to shout for help.

Traveler jumped on him.

He leapt up and onto the man's sternum, at the last moment stomping down in a Special Forces "commando stomp," which smashes the cartilage and bone of the chest, driving splinters through heart and lungs. The man shuddered and lay still.

Traveler unlocked the cell doors, whispering to each group of prisoners, "Wait till we clear the outer office, then come out. Be quiet till then." Then he went to the

150

door to the office, leading the four men he'd selected, plus Thorne, Martin, and Orwell.

Orwell said, "Lemme go first and take the guard out." He patted the breach of the SMG.

Traveler shook his head. "I want things quiet till the last possible moment."

He took a shuriken between thumb and forefinger of his right hand and unlocked the door with the keys in his left. He pushed the door open and stepped through, raising the shuriken.

But the guard was sitting at a desk opposite the door. He looked up as Traveler stepped through. The guy had good reflexes. He instantly snatched up the submachine gun lying on the desktop and slapped at the safety. He aimed and squeezed the trigger—as Traveler's shuriken-throwing star flashed through the air and found its mark, sinking its tooth in the man's brain.

But not before the guard squeezed off a burst of 9mm rounds at the door.

Traveler flung the star—and flung himself aside. The burst smashed into the wall and the metal door. No one was hit.

But getting to his feet, Traveler heard a clatter of footsteps on the stairway. Someone had heard and was coming to investigate.

"Did you hear something?" Wentworth asked.

He was standing by the window of Vallone's admin building office. Vallone was sitting at the desk. Jan stood before the desk, arms crossed over her chest. The room was almost barren; there was a steel desk, a chair behind it, a chair facing it—which Jan had refused—and a single window. Bare wooden walls, recently painted army green.

"No, I didn't hear anything," Vallone said, annoyed at the interruption.

"It was a rattling sound."

"That's probably what you heard: a rattling sound. Which could be ten million things." He returned his attention to Jan. "What was it you were asking me? Oh, yes, why are the cells so crowded. And what do we do with the prisoners. As for the crowding, it's temporary. This is a sort of clearinghouse for the draftees. Once a week a truck comes from one of our salvage camps or our other bases and picks up a few. All prisoners are brought here first. Some are used as labor force, in construction or clearing rubble at salvage sites. Others are used according to their special skills—with close supervision. Others are given to the labs. I suspect you're thinking that if you don't get your brother out by dealing with us, your tribe can waylay some convoy taking him to his assignment. Right? You can forget it. He's special. He isn't going to leave here alive unless you tell us where we can find the other NT77 storage dump. It's as simple as that—"

He broke off, frowning. "I did hear something. Sounded like gunfire."

Vallone got up and went to the window; he and Wentworth looked out the window at the detention center.

Jan smiled.

They'd turned their back on her because she was a woman. They therefore considered her to be no great danger to them. Men were always making that mistake.

She moved silently up behind them, snatched the pistol from Vallone's belt, and took a step back out of reach. As they turned, she checked the clip. The gun was ready to fire.

Vallone and Wentworth looked at one another, and then at the gun.

"You're making a stupid mistake," Vallone said. "You'll never get out of here. You and your brother are trapped

"Shit goddamn son of a bitch!" she burst out, watching Vallone go.

"Now, is that ladylike language?" someone said behind her.

She spun and found she was looking into the muzzle of an M16. One-Eye was holding the rifle on her and grinning nastily. "You drop that little popgun there or I'll blow you apart, pretty squaw."

She lowered the gun and let it slip from her fingers.

"That's better. Now, me and you are gonna find us a little car and get away from here and start all over somewhere. Maybe raise us a family. You'll learn to love me, honey. If you don't—I'll sell you. How's that sound, now, huh?"

She shrugged and smiled, moved toward him. "You're really on top of things. I like that. Okay, let's get out of here." She stepped inside the reach of his gun muzzle and reached for him as if she were about to slip her arms around him. He smacked her hard, across the side of the head with the gunbarrel. She grunted and fell over. Blood ran down her cheek from a contusion in her right temple.

"I'm not stupid, little lady. Now get up and get moving. . . ."

She turned to look at him. "Fuck you. I'd rather you shot me."

"Okay, bitch. You get your wish." He pointed the gun at her head.

She didn't hear the shot because of the noise from the firefight on the other side of the camp. Rattle of automatic fire; thump of grenades. But she saw the effect of the shot as One-Eye got a funny look in his one eye, a quizzical, confused sort of look. And then he fell over on his face, sprawled out and dead, a gaping red hole in his back.

Martin ran up, his rifle smoking, and said, "You okay?"

"Yeah—get down!"

157

Half a dozen Glory Boys were running toward them, M16s blazing.

They flung themselves aside, then got up running, making it around a corner just as the enemy got a bead on them. Bullets ripped into the wall. Martin flattened against the wall around the corner from the oncoming Glory Boys. Jan tugged at his arm. "They've got us outgunned! Let's run for it!"

He shook his head. "I owe these morons something."

He took a hand grenade from inside his coat. He waited till he could hear them approaching the corner. Guessed they were ten feet away. He pulled the pin, counted one, two, and tossed it around the corner. It landed in their midst, exploding almost immediately.

Jan and Martin couldn't see what the grenade had done. But a moment later an army helmet rolled on edge, like a rolling coin, around the corner. Trailing blood.

And then: *THOOM*. The ground rocked with an explosion.

"Sounds like Traveler blew up the fuel supply in the nerve-gas building," Martin said. He sighed. "Waste of fuel."

A military truck roared around the corner, coming at them.

Martin swung his rifle toward it, took aim—and lowered it.

Orwell was at the wheel of the truck. Traveler came along behind in the Meat Wagon. There were three other trucks coming. The Meat Wagon pulled up beside Martin and Jan. Traveler got out, ran into the burning building, and came out with his rifles.

They all got in, and the van followed the trucks toward the gate. The remainder of the guards had deserted. Martin and Jan sat up front, crammed in together. Jan let her hand slide over to Traveler's shoulder. They were relieved to see each other alive.

"Vallone got away," she said as they gunned through the shattered gate.

"I know," Traveler said. "I saw the jeep go. But we got Martin out. And we blew Vallone's operation all to hell. And we burned out the NT77."

"Did you salvage any of the fuel?" Martin asked.

Traveler shook his head. "Needed it in there with the nerve gas to make sure the thing burned. Fire neutralizes the nerve gas. Otherwise it'd float up in a cloud—might float to anywhere. Had to burn it out."

"The lights are still on in the camp," Jan said, looking over her shoulder.

Traveler nodded. "We couldn't get to the power line before they sent out a message. There's a chance we could be intercepted by a strike force from Base Zero. . . ."

There were four trucks, collected from around the compound, driven by Slam Sam, Thorne, and other prisoners, up ahead. They were packed with liberated slaves.

They were two miles out from the base when the strike force of Glory Boys appeared, a quarter of a mile to the east, coming to intercept them.

Orwell had taken them to an asphalt highway, leading to the northwest; he was on his way to a kind of refugee camp he knew about, one that had been set up in the ruins of a monastery by a priest and half a dozen aging nuns. The former slaves could reorganize from there. They'd captured a great deal of ammo and other tradables from the detention center. That would give them a chance, somewhere.

Unless the Glory Boys recaptured them.

"Like hell they will," Traveler muttered, swinging off the road, cutting across the desert to intercept the Glory Boys.

The convoy of freed slaves continued on, full speed, hoping to outrun the army.

Martin and Jan each took up an assault rifle and wedged it in a firing slit on the side facing the Glory Boys; Jan in the back now, Martin up front. They were coming at the Glory Boys at a forty-five degree angle, driving hell-bent to cut off their point.

There were about fifty in the strike force; four out front on three-wheeled motorcycles, two in a jeep equipped with a tripod machine gun, the rest, in a double line, rode sloppily behind on horseback. The Glory Boys on vehicles should have held back, remained with the cavalry, Traveler thought. He might be able to get at them in an isolated firefight.

The desert here was almost featureless, gray-white in moonlight and starlight. The army vehicles were lit up by their own headlights. Traveler drove without a light, trusting to luck, swerving around the occasional boulder at the last possible second.

They didn't see him coming until he was almost on top of them.

He angled in on the jeep first, judging it to be the most dangerous. His right hand hovered over the fire button mounted on his steering column until the jeep was in his cone of fire zone. The machine gunner was swiveling to face him when Traveler thumbed the button. The two heavy MGs mounted atop the Meat Wagon chattered, their trajectories coming together to strafe across the jeep as Traveler gunned closer. The machine gun on the jeep spit flame—and then cut off as the gunner was knocked by Traveler's slugs from his perch, sent spinning head over heel into the desert where he lay still as a cast-aside rag doll.

Traveler cut through the line of bikes and swung around back for another pass. He angled out to cut off the motorcycles. He needn't have bothered—they were veer-

160

ing to take him on, coming at him in a flying wedge formation. Guns mounted on their handlebars flared, muzzleflashes strobing, and slugs whined off the Meat Wagon's front-end armoring, or bit into its side and stopped against the bullet-proof vests. Martin and Jan returned fire, automatic rifles thudding repetitively, and one of the bikes exploded, became a rolling ball of flame, then turned over and burned behind the others.

The bikes came head to head with the Meat Wagon, turning aside at the last moment. He struck one glancingly with his right bumper, the van shuddering with the impact. The bike was sent spinning into the darkness, ending as a tangle of twisted metal and broken humanity.

The other two passed the van and swung around to meet it again. The van and the bikes began a sort of square-dance interweaving, circling one another, cutting in and out, all around a central point, dust rising to cloud the stars—and then the horsemen were upon them, cutting off the Meat Wagon's escape, riding around and around it, firing from their saddles, bullets making star patterns on the Meat Wagon's windshields.

Traveler knew he only had a few minutes left. He was surrounded and outgunned. He squeezed the fire button, strafing through a wall of horses and riders, seeing bullet pocks erupt on horseflesh and manflesh alike.

They were too thick around him. He had to stop the van. They rode around them like Indians around a covered wagon. Martin and Jan—actual Indians—fired back at the surrounding cavalry.

And then Danny came, riding in hard with thirty braves.

"Christ, what took him so long?" Traveler muttered.

"There were more before. Someone must have ambushed them," Jan said, sighting through the firing slit. She brought down another Glory Boy with a short burst.

The Indians, Knife Wind's people, slashed in and out of

the ranks of the Glory Boys, guns blazing and arrows winging.

The Glory Boys hadn't seen them coming. They were caught off guard, getting it from the inside, from the Meat Wagon, and from the Indians around them.

They fled with only twenty horsemen. Danny pursued them a way with ten braves while the others finished off the wounded and began to scavenge through the army saddlebags.

"Christ," Traveler said. "The Indians rescued us from the cavalry."